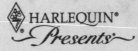

What have we got for you in Harlequin Presents books this month? Some of the most gorgeous men you're ever likely to meet!

With *His Royal Love-Child,* Lucy Monroe brings you another installment in her gripping and emotional trilogy, ROYAL BRIDES; Prince Marcello Scorsolini has a problem—his mistress is pregnant! Meanwhile, in Jane Porter's sultry, sexy new story, *The Sheikh's Disobedient Bride,* Tally is being held captive in Sheikh Tair's harem...because he intends to tame her! If it's a Mediterranean tycoon that you're hoping for, Jacqueline Baird has just the guy for you in *The Italian's Blackmailed Mistress*: Max Quintano, ruthless in his pursuit of Sophie, whom he's determined to bed using every means at his disposal! In Sara Craven's *Wife Against Her Will,* Darcy Langton is stunned when she finds herself engaged to businessman Joel Castille— traded as part of a business merger! The glamour continues with *For Revenge...Or Pleasure?*—the latest title in our popular miniseries FOR LOVE OR MONEY, written by Trish Morey, truly is romance on the red carpet! If it's a classic read you're after, try *His Secretary Mistress* by Chantelle Shaw. She pens her first sensual and heartwarming story for the Presents line with a tall, dark and handsome British hero, whose feisty yet vulnerable secretary tries to keep a secret about her private life that he won't appreciate.

Check out www.eHarlequin.com for a list of recent Presents books! Enjoy!

Amanda Browning

THE LAWYER'S CONTRACT MARRIAGE

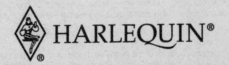

HARLEQUIN®

TORONTO • NEW YORK • LONDON
AMSTERDAM • PARIS • SYDNEY • HAMBURG
STOCKHOLM • ATHENS • TOKYO • MILAN • MADRID
PRAGUE • WARSAW • BUDAPEST • AUCKLAND

ISBN 0-373-18875-7

THE LAWYER'S CONTRACT MARRIAGE

First North American Publication 2006.

This edition published by arrangement with Harlequin Books S.A.

® and TM are trademarks of the publisher. Trademarks indicated with
® are registered in the United States Patent and Trademark Office, the
Canadian Trade Marks Office and in other countries.

www.eHarlequin.com

Printed in U.S.A.

All about the author...
Amanda Browning

AMANDA BROWNING is still happily single and lives in
the old family home on the borders of Essex. She enjoys
her extended family and is the great-aunt to eighteen nieces
and nephews. She especially enjoys her twin sister's two
grandchildren, one who's very close, and she risks serious
damage to her back when playing the fool with them!

She began writing romances when she left her job at the
library and wondered what to do next. She remembered a
colleague once told her to write a romance, and went for
it. Her first effort elicited an invitation to visit Mills & Boon
headquarters. Although her first two manuscripts could not
be used, the third was accepted and she hasn't looked back
since.

Besides writing, which occupies a great deal of her time,
she is very interested in researching her family tree. This has
led to discovering relatives in the United States and Canada,
and just recently these relations have visited the U.K. She
is about to plunge into the world of the Internet in order
to make more discoveries, which should be interesting in
more ways than one!

What is left of her spare time is spent doing counted cross-
stitch, and she really enjoys the designs based on the works
of Marty Bell, as well as the gorgeous designs of Victorian
Ladies, angels by Lavender & Lace, and Mirabilia ranges—
they are so intricate. She finds it very satisfying to finish one
and finally see it hanging on a wall.

Of course, she still manages to find time for some
gardening. Like most gardeners, she is constantly waging
war against cats, who think the beds are their private
toilets, and the snails, who dine out on her flowers. So far
she has resisted the ultimate deterrent of trekking out at
night with a torch and a bucket, but she's giving it serious
consideration!

CHAPTER ONE

SAM LOMBARDI knew, without the shadow of a doubt, that she couldn't possibly be any happier. It was early morning, the time of day she most enjoyed, and she was lying in the arms of the man she loved. Ransom Shaw. Just thinking his name gave her an enormous sense of well-being. Sighing with satisfaction, she smiled, cuddling closer, taking in the scent of him as his chest rose and fell whilst he slept.

She might be just a little biased, but she thought he was perfect. Simply looking at him turned her heart over. He was ruggedly handsome, with a shock of black hair that just curled over his collar, contrary to current fashion, and dancing grey eyes set in a tanned face. Right now that tanned face bore a night's growth of stubble, which just made him look sexier so far as she was concerned.

She toyed with the idea of waking him and initiating the lovemaking that would surely follow, but decided he could do with the sleep. He was a struggling junior barrister in a prestigious law firm, and had been working hard on his latest case. He was hoping to progress to being a senior barrister, and to one day take silk. It was going to take hard work, but he had the ability to get what he wanted.

Sam had actually met Ransom when she had been called in to act as interpreter in connection with his current case. There had been instant attraction. She had never experienced anything like it. They had been drawn to each other so powerfully, nobody else existed. Within days they had been lovers, and nothing had ever seemed so right. For her it wasn't an affair, it was for ever. A for ever kind of love.

She had no doubts. This was it. He was the one. She had fallen fathoms deep in love with him, and was sure it was true for Ransom too.

The days had turned into weeks. Now weeks were slipping into months, and their feelings had simply gone from strength to strength. They were soul mates, destined to be together...

Beneath her cheek his chest expanded as he breathed in deeply. Sam glanced up to find his enticing grey eyes looking down at her. Ransom smiled slowly.

'Hey,' he greeted softly, running his hand over the silky undulations of her back.

Sam moved so that she was resting on his chest and could look down at him. 'Hi. Did I disturb you?' she asked equally gently, and his smile took on a rakish curve.

'You always disturb me, I'm happy to say,' Ransom responded teasingly, and she could feel his body hardening beneath her thigh.

Sam laughed softly and pressed a chain of kisses from shoulder to shoulder. 'You shouldn't be doing this. You need your sleep.'

Ransom's answer to that was to fold his arms around her and roll over so their positions were reversed. 'I need you more,' he told her huskily, no longer smiling, and the heat in his gaze was enough to set her blood boiling. 'God, I'm totally crazy about you.'

'How can I resist you when you say something like that?' Sam murmured on a sigh, and then his head lowered, blocking out the light, and all sensible thought was forgotten in the heat of passion.

Much later, having taken a leisurely shower before dressing, they sat facing each other across the breakfast bar in Ransom's flat. Sam buttered a hot piece of toast and hastily plopped it onto his plate before it could burn her. She did another for herself and spread it with marmalade.

'Are you in court today?' she queried, wondering if they could manage to snatch a quick lunch together. It wasn't always easy fitting in with his gruelling schedule.

Ransom nodded as he sipped at a steaming cup of coffee. 'Closing arguments. It's probably going to be a long day. How about you?'

Sam worked for a company that supplied translators for every possible occasion or event. She was fluent in half a dozen languages, and could get by in a handful of others. Which kept her busy and was never boring.

'I'll call the office from home to find out what's lined up for me.' She had to go to her own bedsit to change her clothes and check her mail.

Having finished his breakfast, Ransom carried his dirty crocks to the sink, then shrugged into the jacket of his pinstripe suit. 'Dinner tonight?'

Regretfully, Sam shook her head. 'Can't, I'm afraid. I'm having dinner with my family.' It had been her custom ever since she had moved into her own place, and she had never felt torn about where she wanted to be until now.

'When am I going to meet this family of yours?' Ransom wanted to know. He had asked more than once recently and Sam wasn't quite sure why she was putting it off.

'Soon,' she promised. She supposed she just wanted to keep him to herself for a while longer. If she took him home, the speculation would start. She loved her family dearly, but sometimes she felt she could be smothered under their natural interest in all her doings.

Ransom quirked an eyebrow at her. 'Are you ashamed of me or something?'

That brought her to her feet in a hurry. 'No, of course not!' The fact was she had never taken a man home, and her family would know the significance when she did. 'I just don't want to share you yet.' Ransom would get the third degree, and she needed to prepare him for it first.

He smiled lazily. 'That's OK, just so long as you remember I'm going to have to meet them one day.'

Smiling with relief, Sam went and slipped her arms around his neck. 'One day. We're OK just the two of us till then, aren't we?'

His hands settled on her waist and drew her closer. 'Two is good. Forget I mentioned it. I'm just an old-fashioned kind of guy about some things. It'll keep,' he reassured her, just before pressing a scintillating kiss on her lips.

It was over much too soon for Sam, who sighed when he released her to go in search of his briefcase. Still, what he had said gave her a warm feeling. There really was only one reason for an old-fashioned kind of man to want to meet a woman's parents: to show his intentions were honourable. She smiled to herself. There was nothing she wanted more than to marry Ransom Shaw and spend the rest of their lives together. Maybe she would take him home soon after all.

'What are you dreaming about?' Ransom asked laughingly, jerking her out of her reverie, and Sam felt colour wash into her cheeks.

She could hardly tell him that she was thinking wistfully of the idea that he might be going to propose. 'Oh, just that you're one heck of a kisser!' she retorted lightly, gathering up the tiny handbag she had brought with her last night. 'Did you get a lot of practice?'

Grey eyes glittered. 'It only feels this good because you're kissing the right person.'

'And you know this because…?' she prompted and he laughed huskily.

'OK, OK. I know it because I've kissed a lot of wrong ones. Happy now?'

She laughed as her inner happiness overflowed. 'Ecstatically happy. I go around with a permanent grin on my face these days. People will begin to think I'm crazy.'

'Just tell them you're crazy about me. That will explain everything.'

As they left the flat Sam silently agreed that it certainly would.

The rest of the day was boringly normal. After Ransom dropped her off, Sam changed into her work clothes, rang the office to check the jobs she had to do, then drove herself to her first appointment. From that moment she barely stopped to breathe, so it was a surprise to glance at her watch and see how late it was. So she abandoned the idea of going home to change, and instead drove directly to her parents' house.

She knew something was wrong the instant she walked inside the front door. Usually her family would be gathered round the large dining table, noisily passing on their bits and pieces of news. This time, however, her brothers and sisters were in the sitting room, talking in hushed voices. They all glanced up when she entered, and Sam could see there were notable absences. The other halves and their children were missing. Something unheard of for family night.

'Where is everybody?' she asked, and all at once her sisters began sobbing whilst her brothers looked grim. 'What's going on?' she added, dropping her things in the nearest chair.

Her eldest brother Tom had clearly been appointed spokesman. 'We've been waiting for you to get here. Mum and Dad are in the kitchen. They'll tell you everything.'

Sam frowned. 'Why can't you tell me? And where's Tony?' she added, having realised her second-eldest brother was missing too.

'Go see the parents, Sam. You should hear it from them,'

Tom insisted, and, feeling as if a lump of lead had settled in her stomach, Sam headed for the kitchen.

Her parents were seated at the kitchen table. Her mother had clearly been crying, and was tearing a tissue to shreds in silent anguish. Her father, by contrast, was silent, but his complexion was so pale he looked ill. They, too, looked up when she walked in, but when neither rose to greet her she knew the situation was serious.

'What is it? What's wrong?' she asked with a sick feeling of dread growing inside her.

Her mother stifled a sob behind the mutilated tissue and rose to her feet, walking to the sink and gripping the edge till her knuckles grew white. Sam looked from one to the other, seeking answers. Finally her father swallowed hard and turned to her.

'Sit down, Sam. We've got a problem. A very serious one,' he admitted in a broken voice, and Sam sat down opposite him, pressing a hand over his as they lay on the tabletop.

'What kind of problem? Has Tony done something?' Her brother was the wild one of the family. Trouble was his middle name. Over the years he had given his parents more grief than the rest of them put together.

The question produced a wail of anguish from her mother, who instantly stifled it behind both hands.

Her father took a deep breath before revealing the truth. 'Your brother Tony has been caught stealing.'

Sam's heart plummeted. 'What was he stealing?' she asked uneasily, though she had a good idea. Tony was a gambler—an unlucky one.

As if he read her mind, her father nodded. 'Money. A very great deal of money.'

'Can we pay it back?' Sam queried immediately. They had done it before. Surely they could do it again.

'Would that we could, but it's too much this time. Even

if I sold the house and the business, it wouldn't come close
to enough. How can we find this kind of money? Tony will
go to prison and the scandal will kill your mother and ruin
the business,' her father declared in despair.

'Is there nothing we can do?' she asked, appalled to see
her father look so anguished. 'Who does he owe it to?'

Her mother spun round from the sink. 'Don't tell her.
You can't tell her!'

Sam's gaze flickered from one to the other. 'Why not?'

'Because I know what you'll do, and I won't let you!
Why should you have to pay for what Tony has done?' her
mother declared angrily, and Sam's blood ran cold.

'Who did he take the money from, Dad?' she insisted
tensely. 'You might as well tell me. You will in the end.'

Her parents exchanged a look fraught with helplessness.
Finally, though, her mother nodded and her father revealed
the final twist in the tale.

'The Grimaldis.'

Sam caught her breath, for to say the name was to say
all. The Grimaldis were seriously rich, with fingers in many
pies. They had helped her father set up his business many
years ago, and at his request had employed Tony in their
wine import/export business—and he had paid them back
by stealing money to cover his gambling debts. This time
he had screwed up big-time. A bubble of anger surged inside her at the thought that he could do this to his family.

She shot to her feet. 'Where's Tony hiding? I'm going
to kill him for this!' she cried furiously.

Her father caught her hand. 'Sit down, Sam. Tony is at
the Grimaldi house. Nothing has been decided yet.'

Sam subsided, frowning her confusion. 'What is he doing
there? Have the police been called in?'

It took a while for her father to summon the right words,
and when he spoke his voice was scratchy. 'Not yet, and
perhaps never. You see, Sam, the…problem can be made

to vanish without trace, but there is a condition,' he said, keeping his eyes on his clenched fists. 'Leno Grimaldi will replace the money from his personal account...providing you agree to marry him.' With those words her father finally looked at her.

Sam sat back in shock as the words sank in. There was a way out of the terrible mess, but only if she married Leno Grimaldi. She summoned up a mental picture of the man. Leno Grimaldi was some years older than her father. A widower who had had his eye on her ever since she'd turned eighteen. Whilst she knew he had feelings for her, she had never been able to reciprocate. Oh, he was a nice enough man, but way too old for her. She had been careful to keep him at arm's length, and had refused all his attempts to ask her out. Now, thanks to her brother's stupidity, he had the means to get what he wanted. He knew how close their family was, and he was banking on her not being able to let her brother go to gaol, no matter how much Tony deserved it.

Which left Sam in the middle of her worst nightmare. She could save her family from scandal, but only by turning her back on the man that really mattered to her. He was her world, her life. How could she bear to give him up? How could she give up all her hopes and dreams for her brother's indiscretion? Yet how could she do anything else? How could she selfishly put her own needs before those of her family, knowing they were teetering on the brink of ruin and she was the only one who could save them?

Despair sat heavily on her shoulders. There was only one man she wanted to marry, and that was Ransom Shaw. She wanted to cry out that it wasn't fair! She shouldn't have to choose like this! But it was what she was going to have to do.

'Of course we don't expect you to agree to it, my darling,' her mother insisted tearfully. 'We wouldn't ask it of you.'

Her father rose and drew his wife into his arms, comforting her as best he could. 'Your mother's right, Sam. We'll find another way. We only told you because Leno insisted that we do so. He wants you to give him your answer, then matters will proceed from there.'

Sam had to admire Leno Grimaldi's tenacity. He had seen what he wanted and had waited for the opportunity to get it. He must be one hell of a poker player, for he knew to a nicety how to play her. It was to be her choice and her answer, because he knew she couldn't abandon her family to their fate. He probably thought it would be a simple decision, but he didn't know about Ransom. Nobody did. Only her.

'What other way is there? The debt has to be paid off. If you give up your house and business, you'll never be able to raise the money through a loan, or pay off the remainder. Whichever way you look at it, I'm your only hope,' Sam countered with unnatural calmness. 'What happens to Tony if I agree to this?'

'He'll go to live with my cousin in Australia. The sheep station is far enough away from temptation to keep your brother on the straight and narrow,' her father said tiredly. 'Hopefully it will make a man of him.'

'It will do him more good than going to prison,' she agreed, and her mother uttered a tiny cry that Sam responded to with a wry smile. 'It's OK, I haven't decided yet. I must have some time to think about it. How long will Leno wait for my answer?'

'Until this time tomorrow. But there's nothing to think about. You can't do it. I forbid you,' her father commanded gruffly, and Sam silently shook her head.

'Thanks for saying that, but it's my decision.'

'Think of yourself, Sam. Don't worry about us,' her father urged, and she hugged them both.

'I love you. Don't worry,' she advised them, though she knew they would. 'How much do the others know?'

'Only that Tony's in trouble again.'

'Good. Don't say anything yet,' Sam advised with an encouraging smile, not wanting them to know how agonised she was feeling. 'I'd better go. I've got a lot to think about. I'll call you.'

'Don't do anything rash, darling!' her mother called after her, and Sam shook her head.

'I won't,' she said to ease her mother's mind, then headed back to the sitting room. Once again everyone looked up as she came in and gathered up her belongings. 'I have to go. Don't worry about Tony. It's being sorted out.'

'How?' Tom asked tersely as he stood up to confront her. 'What's going on, Sam?'

'He's been gambling again. But as I said, it's being sorted out. I'm off to settle the details now,' she told him, looking round the anxious group of faces and trying to be strong. 'Look after Mum and Dad. They need your support right now.'

They tried to get her to say more, but Sam shook her head and beat a hasty retreat to the front door, where only Tom followed her.

'Are you OK, Sam?' he asked in concern, and it was nearly her undoing. She had to swallow furiously in order to answer.

'I'm fine. Really. I'm furious with Tony, and upset for Mum and Dad, but we'll muddle through as we always do. Now I really must go,' she insisted, and hurried down the path, feeling his eyes on her back all the way.

Feeling as brittle as eggshell, Sam climbed into her car. Knowing that Tom was still watching, she drove off, but, having turned a couple of corners, she pulled the car over and turned off the engine. She sat back, and her head dropped in defeat. What could she do? How could she live with herself if she turned her back on her parents and let them suffer for their wayward son? She wished she could do it, for she didn't want to have to give Ransom up, but it wasn't in her. Her parents had sacrificed so much to give their children a better life, and it was about time someone did something for them. The burden had fallen on her shoulders, and she had to be the one to make the sacrifice.

Her eyes burned with the sting of unshed tears as she thought of what she had to do. It was going to break her heart, but when she told Ransom why she was going to marry Leno Grimaldi she was sure he would understand that she had no choice. Her family had to come first. She drew in a shaky breath. Would it be too much to hope they could part as friends? Honesty forced her to admit it probably was. Life simply didn't work that way.

Yet she couldn't dwell on that and do what she had to do. So she took several deep breaths and pulled herself together. She had things to do, and they would set in motion a course of events that would be irreversible.

Sam knew where Leno Grimaldi lived, and she drove right over there despite the advancing hour. Leno answered the door to her knock himself, and much to her relief he didn't look the least bit smug or self-satisfied. He was politeness itself as he invited her in.

'Sam, my dear, it's so lovely to see you. Come in. Come in. You'll find your brother in the lounge,' he declared warmly, making it seem as if there were nothing out of the ordinary about this visit. 'This way,' he went on, pointing to a half-open door.

When she walked into the extremely elegant room, her brother Tony shot to his feet, looking pale and worried.

'Hi, Sam,' he greeted her, trying to sound cheerful, but it foundered when he met the icy look in her eye.

'Can I get you something to drink?' Leno Grimaldi asked, but Sam shook her head. She hadn't eaten, and alcohol on an empty stomach was inadvisable.

'Thank you, no. I'd better keep a clear head.'

Leno Grimaldi smiled faintly. 'Always wise when talking business,' he agreed easily, indicating she should take a chair opposite her brother.

'Business?' Tony queried, looking from one to the other as they sat down.

'Your sister is here to discuss your future,' Leno explained to him. 'And our own.'

Seeing her brother about to ask more questions, Sam cut him off. 'For once in your life just sit there and be quiet. You've done quite enough,' she snapped at him, then turned to the older man. 'Forgive my bluntness, but I don't think there's anything to be gained by beating about the bush. Is this offer for real? If I marry you, you'll replace the money Tony took?' she asked baldly, and though he winced a little Leno inclined his head.

'It will be my wedding gift to your family,' he confirmed. 'You agree?'

Sam looked at him, seeing a handsome middle-aged man who, for all his good points, was not above using her family's crisis to his own ends. She felt nothing for him, but for her family she would marry the devil himself. 'I agree,' she said flatly, and heard a door slam in her mind, telling her there was no turning back now.

'No, Sam! You can't!' Tony protested, suddenly seeming to realise what was going on. She looked at him, and registered the horror on his face.

'I can and I am. But don't think I'm doing it for you. This is for Mum and Dad. They deserve better than what you were going to put them through,' she told him coldly.

Leno said nothing, merely rose to his feet. 'The money will be replaced in the morning and we will not mention it again. However, there are some papers that I need you all to sign,' he told her as he went to a bureau that stood against the wall and took a sheaf of papers from it.

This was something Sam hadn't expected. 'Papers?'

He smiled at her benignly. 'Nothing serious. I'm sure you can appreciate that it would not be good for business if this incident, and the arrangements made to rectify it, should ever become public knowledge. Therefore this is a simple agreement that you will not tell anyone what has gone on here, with the exception of your parents and your brother. All of you will sign it and be bound by it. No one is to ever speak of it again. Should it get out, the debt will have to be paid in full. It is therefore in your own best interest, and that of your family, to say nothing. Is that understood?'

Sam realised that she should have known Leno would insist on something like this. He was first and foremost a businessman. He would not want this ever getting out, and that meant that she could not now tell Ransom the truth. The implications of that were something she could not think about right that minute. She had given her word and was caught. All she could do was agree and sign on the dotted line. Which she did, and then watched over her brother whilst he did the same.

'Once your parents have signed, that will be that, my dearest Sam,' Leno declared, taking her hand and kissing it gently. 'And I...I promise you that I will do everything in my power to make you as happy as you have made me.'

Sam closed her eyes momentarily, as for a fleeting moment she was made achingly aware of what she would be giving up. However, her family was everything. They needed the help only she could afford them. So she cleared her throat. 'I shall do my best to be a good wife to you,

Leno. However, there is one other thing I would ask of you.'

If he was surprised he did not show it. 'Name it.'

'I would like us to be married as quickly as possible.' Now that she had given her word she did not want to have too much time to think.

Leno smiled and took both of her hands in his this time. 'Ah, we think alike, you and I. I will make the arrangements. Then, after we are married, we will take a long honeymoon in Italy. I have always wanted to go back home one day. I will show you where I grew up. You will love it there.'

Right then Sam didn't know if she would ever care for anything again, but she agreed with his plan. Frankly, it didn't matter where they went or what they did, for she would only be going through the motions. Her life had just changed for ever.

All Sam wanted to do was leave, but she didn't know how to. Having just agreed to marry this man, how could she simply walk out? Whether he realised her discomfort or not, it was Leno who came to her rescue.

'I'm sure you will want to take your brother home and tell your parents what has happened here tonight. We will have dinner together Saturday to discuss our plans, my dear Sam,' he said conversationally as he walked them to the door. 'Ah, and please tell your father I will call on him tomorrow. Good night, my dear,' he added as he bent and kissed her on either cheek.

Sam had braced herself for the brush of his lips on hers, but this he did not do, and she was grateful for his forbearance. 'Good night,' she responded gruffly, and, taking Tony by the arm, hustled him to where she had parked the car.

She drove her brother back to their parents' house, and it was only then that he spoke.

'I'm sorry, Sam,' he apologised. 'I got in over my head and I didn't know what to do.'

Sam looked at his forlorn figure and was torn between justifiable anger and love. 'You were lucky this time, but don't expect that to happen again. You have to stop gambling, Tony, and if that means seeking help, then get it.'

He drew in a shaky breath. 'I will. I promise. Are you coming in?'

She shook her head. 'Not now. You tell Mum and Dad what happened, and what Leno said. I'll phone them tomorrow.'

Tony climbed out, then bent down to look in at her. 'Oh, God, Sam, have I ruined your life?'

Sam felt pain tear through her as she heard his words. Though she felt like crying, she managed to shake her head. 'Hey, you know what they say. Life is what happens whilst you're making other plans. Now go in. Don't keep them worrying any longer. Remember, say nothing to the others.'

'I won't let you down, Sam. I promise,' he told her, then squared his shoulders and went inside.

Alone in the car, Sam closed her eyes for a moment, then put the car in gear and drove off. How could she tell her brother he had ruined her life, even if he had? It wasn't in her nature. All she asked was that he kept his promise. That he came good. For then any sacrifice would have been worth it.

By the time she reached her bedsit, it was late and she was exhausted. It didn't help to have missed a meal, but she didn't feel like eating. Glancing around her, she could see the things she had tossed here and there only that morning when Ransom had dropped her off. Then she had thought the whole of the future was theirs for the taking. Now she knew for ever had been a mere handful of hours.

Sinking onto the lumpy couch, she placed a trembling hand over her heart and could almost feel it breaking.

Ransom. His name was an unremitting ache deep inside. She longed to see him, but dared not. Not until she knew what she was going to do. But she could talk to him. To hear his voice would pour some balm on the open wound where her heart had been.

Reaching for the telephone, she had to swallow hard before she had enough composure to dial his number. When he picked up and growled into the handset, a crystal tear blurred her vision.

'Hi. Did I wake you?' she asked softly, visualising him sitting up in bed and switching on the lamp so he could see the clock.

'Sam? Is everything OK?' Ransom queried immediately, seeing how late it was.

A lump started to grow in her throat, making it hard to speak. 'Um-hmm. I just wanted to hear the sound of your voice.' Had needed it so badly. 'How did it go today?'

'The jury's still out. We're hoping for a result tomorrow. How was dinner with your family?' he asked, stifling a yawn at the same time.

She wanted to cry out that the sky had fallen in, but couldn't. 'Noisy, as usual. I would rather have been with you.' How she wished she had never gone home tonight, but it would only have put off the inevitable. Had she not gone to her parents, then they would certainly have come to her.

'They sound like my kind of people,' he said, and she could hear the humour in his tone. 'Next time I'll join you, then you won't have to miss me.'

The tear overflowed down her cheek. 'I like the sound of that,' she agreed, whilst her heart contracted at the knowledge that there would be no next time.

'God, I wish you were with me right now. This bed is too damn big and lonely without you in it,' Ransom told her gruffly, and Sam hastily stifled a sob behind her hand.

'It's only one night,' she pointed out when she was able to control her voice. She hated herself for lying, but there was nothing else she could do. She realised now that calling him had been a mistake. She was going to feel worse, not better.

'I guess you're right. To make up for it, have lunch with me tomorrow. I can't go the better part of forty-eight hours without seeing you,' he urged and though she knew it probably wasn't wise, she held onto the lifeline he threw her.

'Lunch would be lovely. Name the place and time and I'll be there,' she promised. It would be all right. By then she should have decided how she was going to break off their affair. Lunch would be a final good memory. She would need all of those she could get.

Ransom named a restaurant close to the court, and she agreed to meet him at the time he suggested. He yawned again, and she knew she had to go. 'I'll let you get back to sleep now.'

'I'm glad you rang. 'Night, sweetheart.'

'Good night, Ransom,' she said back, and held the receiver to her ear until she heard the sound of his phone going down.

Hugging the phone to her chest, she finally gave way to tears. They carried with them a wealth of helplessness. Of loss and utter despair. They tolled out the knell of her dreams, and the prospect of a future that promised to be bleak and empty without the man she loved in it.

CHAPTER TWO

SAM sat at a small table set in the restaurant's window embrasure and waited for Ransom to arrive. Her watch told her he was a little late, but she wasn't worried yet. It wasn't easy to get away from the court on time. She felt…strangely numb. Which was odd, because between crying and thinking she hadn't got much sleep last night.

Thinking of that, she reached into her handbag for a mirror to check her appearance. Thankfully the puffiness around her eyes had gone, and any redness had been hidden by make-up. She looked normal, which was all she could hope for. The numbness was welcome, but it would wear off all too soon. All she asked was that it would last the day out.

Sighing, she rested her chin on her linked fingers and stared at the world passing by outside. She had spent the night refining the details of how she would break things off with Ransom. She had been prohibited from telling the truth, so her options were limited. Of course, she could declare baldly that she didn't want to see him any more, but Ransom was not the kind of man to accept that without a good reason. In the cold light of dawn, she had known that she would have to end their relationship in such a way that he would not want to see her again. The only way to do that was to make him hate her. However, she would only be able to put on a creditable performance once, so she had to get it right the first time.

Hands on her shoulders made her jump and look up. Ransom stood there, smiling down at her, and as her heart turned over he stooped and pressed a kiss to her startled lips.

'You were miles away. What were you dreaming about?' he asked her as he sat down opposite. Reaching across the table, he took one of her hands and held it between his own.

Sam gave a little shrug. 'Nothing, really. Just this and that.'

One eyebrow quirked. 'And here I was thinking you were dreaming about me.'

He made her smile, something she hadn't felt like doing all morning. Lord, but she was going to miss him so much. 'I don't want you to get big-headed.'

Ransom grinned wickedly. 'Meaning you think I'm perfect as I am? Well, now, I can't argue with that.' He stared at her, taking in every feature, and shook his head. 'You are *so* beautiful. I can't get over how beautiful you are.'

Sam uttered a tiny laugh, amazed at how easily he could take her breath away. 'I'm not beautiful.' She considered herself ordinary. There was nothing special about a swathe of silver-blonde hair and a pair of large blue eyes. Not having a vain bone in her body, she thought of herself as moderately attractive rather than beautiful. Her bones were fine, but her features were cool rather than animated. She had no idea that her smile transformed her face, making many a man do a double take. As for her figure, she had always considered that average at best. She went in and out in the right places, but a model she was not.

'You are to me,' he contradicted, holding her gaze with his intense one.

'You're only saying that because you think it will get you somewhere,' she teased him back, whilst inside she could sense the numbness melting away.

Laughing, he released her hand and picked up the menu. 'You're right, young woman. I have definite plans for you.'

'Oh, yes? I'll have to check my diary to see if I'm available,' Sam replied, feeling her heart squeeze tightly.

'You will be,' he told her confidently.

His confidence was unbearably painful, and Sam stared down at her own menu, though the words were unfocussed. She had planned to tell him goodbye here, where the restraints of being in public would limit what he could say, but she knew she couldn't do it. The numbness was wearing off second by second now that he was here. Everything he said had her control slipping, so if she tried to reject him she would only end up in tears and that would never do. It was the wrong moment. She had to regroup and try again another time.

'I've been thinking,' Ransom broke into her troubled thoughts, and she looked up to find him watching her over the top of his menu. 'I have some leave left, and you must have some too. Why don't we go off together for a week? We could drive down to the coast and I can initiate you into the joys of sailing. What do you think?'

'I didn't know you were a sailor,' Sam remarked in surprise.

Ransom grinned. 'You don't know everything about me yet,' he teased. 'If you must know, I could sail before I could walk, so my mother tells me. I love it, but I don't have a boat of my own yet. One day I will, then we'll sail off around the world together and not come back until we're good and ready. What do you say?'

It was a wonderful dream, and she only wished she would be sharing it with him. 'It sounds perfect, but we should try the week first in case I turn out to be a bad sailor.'

'That's a deal, then,' he declared happily, and returned to studying the dishes on offer. 'What are you having?' he asked, and Sam forced herself to focus on the menu.

'A pasta salad, I think,' she decided. Something light that wouldn't choke her when she tried to swallow.

'Mmm, I've a fancy for pasta myself. What if we—?' Whatever he was about to say ended abruptly as the beeper he carried with him went off. 'Damn,' he muttered under his breath as he pulled it from his jacket pocket and studied it. When he glanced up, his expression was rueful. 'Sorry, darling, but I've got to go. It's from Ian, which means the jury must be coming back. Listen, you're having dinner with me tonight. Eight o'clock my place. Don't be late!' he commanded, leaving her no time to argue as he stood up, kissed her quickly then hurried to the door and was gone.

Sam let out a shaky breath and sank back in her seat. This was awful. Here he was making plans for a future they would never have, and she hadn't had the strength to tell him. Tonight she would have to be firm, for it wasn't fair to him. She had to nip everything in the bud before it went too far. The prospect took away what was left of her appetite, so she dropped some money on the table and left. A condemned person, she was coming to realise, rarely ate a hearty meal.

That evening she drove herself to Ransom's flat in a mood of steely resolve. She had spoken to her parents that morning and resisted all their attempts to persuade her to change her mind. When she contacted them again later, they had signed the agreement, and arrangements were already being made for Tony to go and stay with relatives in Australia. Which left only herself with unfinished business.

Of course, it would probably have been easier to simply phone him and say she couldn't see him any more, but that seemed like the coward's way out. He deserved she should tell him to his face. What she said would have to give him no room for hope, because there wasn't any. Sam knew that the best she could do for him now would be to make him never want to see her again. She had to think only of causing him the least pain, not on shielding herself.

Ransom took a moment or two to answer the door, and she had to smile when he did. He was wearing jeans and a shirt with the sleeves rolled up. Around his waist he had tucked a tea towel, and she realised he was cooking dinner himself. A curl of hair had fallen over his forehead, and to Sam he looked endearingly handsome.

He, in turn, looked her over and she saw the flicker of flame in his eyes. Clearly he liked what he saw. She had chosen to wear a sapphire-blue lacy top to match her eyes and black evening trousers to seduce him. It had been important to make herself look good for the task ahead of her. It was meant as a confidence booster.

'I don't know whether to eat dinner or you,' he declared huskily as he shut the door with one hand and pulled her against him with the other. His arms tightened around her as he lowered his head and kissed her.

Though it wasn't what she had planned, Sam couldn't help but kiss him back in silent desperation. One kiss was not enough, and as others followed passion deepened. As their teeth nipped and tongues duelled and incited, she could feel her body turning molten with desire. She wanted him so badly and needed him so very much, and yet she dared not go further. It wouldn't be fair or right.

A thought that finally gave her the strength to break off their kiss and ease herself to arm's length. 'You invited me here for dinner, not to be dinner, remember,' she told him in a breathless voice, knowing she looked thoroughly kissed.

He lifted his hands to her shoulders, his smile rueful. 'You can think of food at a time like this?'

Sam glanced towards the kitchenette and wrinkled her nose. 'I think you should too. Something's starting to burn.'

Ransom released her immediately and hurried into the small kitchen. He removed a frying pan from the heat and checked the contents. 'It's OK. Just a little singed around the edges. It's your fault for making me forget about everything else,' he called back to her.

Sam was eying the table he had set. There were napkins and crystal glasses. Two perfect rosebuds and candles. To even an untutored eye, this was a special occasion. 'What are we celebrating?' she asked curiously, then a thought struck her. 'Of course. You won the case.'

Ransom came back into the room carrying a bowl of salad, which he set on the table. 'That too,' he confirmed. 'Light the candles, would you?' he said before vanishing again.

She did as he asked, telling herself it would be churlish to leave so soon. The case was important to him. The least she could do was celebrate its successful outcome. Then she would do what she had come to do and leave. Inside she knew she was putting off the dreaded moment to the last minute, but she couldn't help it. Just a few more hours wouldn't hurt, surely.

It was a bittersweet time, when she shared Ransom's moment of glory. They laughed and chatted, and toasted his success with a bottle of fine white wine. The evening fairly flew by, and when Ransom went to make the coffee Sam knew she had done herself no favours by staying, yet she couldn't regret it. So she smiled at him when he returned and enjoyed these final fleeting moments of happiness.

Sam would never remember what she was laughing at when she suddenly realised he was quietly sitting there staring at her as if she was the most precious thing he had ever come across. The laughter died away as their eyes met.

'Marry me,' Ransom said simply, and the two words sent her world spinning.

'What?' she asked faintly, not believing she could have heard correctly.

His lips quirked with mild amusement, though his eyes said he was deadly serious. 'I said marry me. I'm asking you to be my wife, Sam.'

The confirmation sent savage fingers to tear at her heart. She was stunned into silence, choked by the knowledge that this was the moment she had longed for. All she wanted was to say yes and spend the rest of her life with him, but with a sinking heart she knew that she had just been given the perfect moment to tear their relationship to shreds.

Knowing hesitation would be fatal, she started to laugh. 'You're joking, right?' Shaking her head, she placed a hand over her heart. 'Boy, you had me going there for a minute.' Whilst Ransom sat there in total shock, she pressed home her advantage. 'I'm not interested in marriage and all that commitment stuff right now.' Reaching for a bread stick, she nibbled on it, though it almost choked her.

Ransom finally recovered enough to react. 'What the hell are you talking about?' he charged, with what she considered justifiable outrage.

'I'm glad we're getting this out into the open now. The truth is I don't want to be tied down,' Sam continued in the same vein, whilst her heart began to beat faster and faster.

'Cut it out. This isn't the time to fool around,' Ransom ordered sharply. 'I love you, Sam, and I know you love me.' She could see the instant he had said it that doubt crept in. 'Or are you telling me it was all a lie?'

'Well, of course I love you, Ransom. You're a very handsome man, and the sex is fantastic, but...' She pretended to notice the look on his face for the first time. Her hand went to her throat. 'Oh, my God, you *were* serious!'

Ransom went very still. All that she could see moving

was the pulse at the base of his throat. 'What's going on, Sam?'

It tore her apart to see the pain replace happiness in his eyes. 'Nothing, I swear. We just seem to have got our lines crossed. I'm so sorry, Ransom, but surely you knew I was only after a good time?'

A nerve ticked in his jaw. 'A good time?' he repeated tersely.

She swallowed hard, but managed to smile encouragingly at him. 'You know the sort of thing. Dinner, the theatre. Mind-blowing sex.'

That produced a shake of his head. 'Pull the other leg, sweetheart. I never got that message from you, ever.'

Of course he hadn't. She loved him, damn it. But it was over, so she sent him an old-fashioned look. 'Well, I could hardly come across that shallow if I wanted the good times to last, could I? I'm sorry if you read it wrong, but the truth is, if it's marriage you want, you had better look for another woman.'

She pushed herself up on legs that trembled badly and went to where she had left her jacket, holding it over her arm before her like a shield. Her heart ached at the coldness that had settled over his face. 'I think it would be best if I left now.' She hesitated, wanting to plead with him not to hate her, but it was that hatred that would help him get over her, so in the end all she said was a husky, 'Bye, darling. Maybe I'll see you around some day,' and let herself out of the flat.

There were simply not enough words in any language to describe how she felt then. What meagre defences she had been able to erect crumbled to nothing. Pain surged in like a tidal wave, and for long minutes she was unable to move. Only the fear that Ransom might find her there gave her the strength to stumble downstairs and out to her car. She fought tears all the way home, and it was nothing less than a miracle that she didn't have an accident. Once indoors she succumbed to her overwhelming misery and cried long into the night.

Somewhere around dawn she finally fell into an uneasy sleep.

A state she was dragged from by the sound of someone pressing their finger on the bell of her bedsit and keeping it there. In no mood for inconsiderate delivery men, she stomped to the door to deliver a heartfelt warning, and was dumbfounded to find Ransom on her doorstep. Having told herself she would not see him again after last night, she was too surprised to prevent him brushing past her and striding into her tiny living room.

One glance at his rigid back warned her he was here to demand further explanation. She hadn't allowed for that, and the bottom fell out of her stomach. Following him into the room, she finger-combed her hair and braced herself for what was to come. He turned to meet her, and looking at his face nearly undid her. He looked grey and haggard, the patent result of a sleepless night. She wanted to reach out to comfort him, but that would only defeat her object. All she could do was keep to her plan, so she folded her arms and sighed testily.

'Honestly, Ransom, couldn't this have waited?' To her own ears she sounded bored, and she was amazed at her acting ability.

'No,' he growled fiercely. 'I want an explanation for what happened last night!'

Of course he did, but she was prevented from giving him the true one. She had to bluff it out as best she could. 'You asked me to marry you, I said no.'

An answer that had his teeth grinding angrily. 'There's more to it than that. I'm not such a bad judge of people. I know we want the same things. To be a family, have children, grow old together,' he charged.

Sam could feel the powerful emotions seething inside him, and wondered if she would ever be able to forgive herself for what she was putting him through. She only knew she couldn't think of another way of doing this.

'Oh, come on, Ransom, you don't believe everything you hear, do you? OK, I might have said it, but not seriously. A person says a lot of things when they want to keep a man happy. I was onto a good thing, so what if I told you a few white lies? The truth is I don't want a husband or family. You've picked the wrong woman for that,' she told him, pretending to stifle a yawn. Then, as a master stroke, she closed the gap between them and started playing with the button of his leather jacket. 'However, I'd be happy for things to stay as they are, if you want.'

He brushed her hand away with a look of utter disgust. 'No, thanks, not even as a gift. You played me for a fool, Sam, but not any more. Fool me once, shame on you. Fool me twice, shame on me. I want nothing more to do with you.'

Fighting back tears, she managed to produce a fatalistic sigh. 'You win some, you lose some. Take care of yourself, Ransom. It's a jungle out there.'

He stared at her for a moment or two longer, a nerve ticking away in his jaw, then he pointed a warning finger at her. 'You'd better not try this on anyone else, darling. They might not be as forbearing as I am. I only want to kill you, they might try to do it.'

With that he slammed out of her bedsit and her life. She was left staring at the door, tears finally streaming down her cheeks.

'I love you,' she whispered achingly as her heart shattered into a thousand irretrievable pieces. Her only solace was in knowing she had done the right thing. He might hate her now, but he would get over it. As for herself, she knew she never would.

*   *   *

In the next few days Sam cried over Ransom until at last she was all cried out, and then she papered over the cracks and faced up to the future without him. Her family closed ranks behind her. Those who didn't know the truth, and were surprised by her decision to marry Leno Grimaldi, followed their parents' line and said nothing.

When she dined with Leno that Saturday evening, she discovered that he had plans for a big wedding. She would have preferred something less elaborate, but fell in with his wishes because he genuinely thought he was giving her something she would enjoy. She did try to protest when he took her to an expensive jeweller's and picked out an engagement ring for her. The large diamond was far too ostentatious, but Leno declared he wanted nothing but the best for her, so she gave in. When it came to the matching wedding bands, she simply went along without fuss, not having the heart to argue any more.

The surprise engagement party, celebrated at a top London hotel, was an evening she battled through with a plastic smile tacked to her lips. She hadn't realised just how important a man Leno was until that night, when the press were there to take countless photos of the soon to be happy couple for the avid readers of their magazines and society pages.

Whatever Leno wanted happened like magic. As soon as a wedding date was set, he arranged for a top designer to make her dress. Sam stumbled through the arrangements, trying to fit shopping trips around her job, but finally she had to give that up. Gifts rained in from right and left, until she wanted to scream that it wasn't real. Yet it was very real, and Sam made a conscious decision not to think ahead to after the wedding, when she and Leno would finally be alone together as husband and wife.

A week away from the wedding, Sam escaped from the

final fitting of her wedding dress and knew she just had to get a few moments of peace or she would go crazy. She and Ransom had loved walking in Kensington Gardens, and suddenly she just had to go there. To be somewhere where she had been happy. Seconds later she was hailing a passing taxi.

As soon as she started walking along the pathways Sam felt as if she could breathe again. Peace settled around her, and after a while she spied an empty seat and sat down. Everything was so normal here, she thought. Unlike her life, which was like a runaway train. Closing her eyes, she allowed the peace and tranquillity to soothe her battered soul.

She was unaware that someone had sat down at the other end of the seat until they spoke.

'So, it wasn't actually marriage you were against, it was the lack of wealth of the man doing the asking,' Ransom declared cuttingly, and Sam's heart lurched as her eyes shot open and she stared at him in shock.

'Where did you come from?' she gasped out, wondering if she had somehow magicked him up.

His smile was chilly. 'I was passing by when I saw you get out of the taxi, so I followed you. I wanted to congratulate you on your forthcoming marriage.'

Somehow she had believed that he would never know about it. She should have known better. 'How did you find out?'

'A colleague of mine saw one of the newspaper articles and recognised your name. He thought I might be interested,' Ransom explained with a mocking laugh. 'You made quite a fetching couple. Shame he's old enough to be your father, but what the hell? He's loaded, so it's a perfect match!'

Sam swallowed hard, unable to voice the lie and say that she cared for Leno. She did, however, raise her chin and stare him out. 'I can marry who I like, and for whatever reason I like.'

Ransom laughed coldly. 'And he has several million reasons for you to like him.'

'I'm not marrying him for his money,' she put in swiftly, though in a roundabout way she was. She just hadn't known quite how wealthy Leno was.

'Pardon me if I don't believe you. I think I was lucky not being rich enough for your taste. I wonder how long it would have taken me to realise it wasn't me you loved, but my money?' Ransom shot back with withering scorn. 'Perhaps I ought to put him straight on a few things.'

The suggestion had her heart leaping into her throat. The last thing she wanted was for Leno to meet Ransom. 'That won't be necessary,' she countered in a strangled voice. 'Leno and I have an understanding.'

Ransom's beautiful eyes were full of dislike as he looked at her. 'I get it. He has his trophy wife and you get to spend his money. How did I ever think I could love you? You two deserve each other!'

Every word he uttered struck home with devastating accuracy and drew blood. If he hadn't hated her enough before, he certainly did now. She had no defence except not to let him see how he had hurt her.

'Have you finished?' she asked him with deceptive calm.

Ransom looked her up and down as if he had never seen her before. 'My God, you're a cool customer. Nothing reaches you, does it? It's OK, darling, I'm done. I wish you joy of your fortune. May it keep you warm at night.'

With those parting words Ransom got up and walked away. Sam knew he never looked back, because she kept her eyes on him till he was out of sight. This time she didn't cry, for the hurt went too deep. She stared unseeingly at the beauty around her and laid the first stones of the wall of ice that would eventually surround her heart and keep it safe. After all, it held her most precious possession: her love for him.

When she finally began to retrace her steps, she did so with her feelings securely encased in ice and a determination to never look back. Whatever happened from this moment, nothing would touch her, neither hurt nor joy, for those were things of the past and that was gone for ever.

CHAPTER THREE

SAM watched the charming Norfolk scenery pass by outside the car and gave a sigh of satisfaction. Not to put too fine a point on it, she was happy, and that was something she had never thought she would be again. Of course she wasn't ecstatically happy, but she knew she would never feel anything close to that again. Nevertheless, she was content.

When her husband Leno had suddenly died of a heart attack six months ago, she had found herself at a crossroads. She hadn't been back to England in over six years. What had begun as a honeymoon trip had ended as a permanent removal. Sam had fully expected to remain in Italy, where the people, and Leno's family in particular, had been kind to her.

She had done all she could to be a good wife, and, because Leno had been a good man, their marriage had not been a total disaster. He had showered her with gifts to mark his deep affection for her, introducing her to a lifestyle she had never dreamed of. His only sadness had been the lack of children. Sam had done nothing to prevent it, it was just not meant to be. Which was a shame, because Leno would have showered them with love too.

He had been good to her, and she had mourned him. Because of the situation regarding their marriage, she had not expected to inherit the bulk of his fortune, but so it had turned out to be. He had no children, and his nearest relatives were cared for, leaving her what remained. It was then that Sam had decided to come home. She knew she had more money than she could ever spend, and that she could have more than enough to live on and still put the rest to good use.

Which was the reason she was a passenger in this powerful convertible car today.

Alex Hunt, the man behind the wheel, knew all the twists and turns of the road they were travelling along very well, for he was taking her to visit his parents. This was Sam's fifth visit, and she looked forward to it, for she got on well with David and Ellen Hunt. The Grimaldi Foundation, which Sam had set up in her husband's name, was helping to fund the building of a new hospice. It was the foundation's first project, and Sam was keeping a finger on the pulse, hence the regular visits.

Alex steered the car around a sharp bend, and Sam watched him manoeuvre the vehicle with ease, her lips curving into a wry smile. She hadn't known him long, but they had quickly become friends. Despite turning thirty a couple of months ago, he had a boyish enthusiasm for fast cars.

He must have felt her eyes on him, for he glanced round at her with a grin. 'What are you smiling at?' he asked lazily, whilst returning his attention to a particularly tricky section of road.

Sam laughed. 'Actually, I was thinking you love your car more than a woman.'

His response was to make a Gallic sound in his throat. '*Mais, non!* You know I love you like crazy, Sam.'

It was only a joke, but for a moment her head was filled with the sound of another voice telling her he loved her, and her heart tightened painfully. Then she ruthlessly quashed the memory, for it had no place in the here and now.

She laughed teasingly. 'Boy, would you run a mile if I took you seriously!'

'You've got that right!' he agreed immediately, returning

his attention to the road as yet another tricky corner came along.

Hoping this good feeling would last, she once more gazed out of the side window. Idly her thumb toyed with her wedding and engagement rings. She still wore them. Not because they meant something to her, but because it kept unwanted interest at bay. She was not in the market for emotional complications.

Studying her reflection, Sam barely recognised the twenty-eight-year-old woman who had loved only one man in her life, and who had married another. Her hair was fashionably cut, she wore expensive clothes and jewellery, and could hold her own amongst the glitterati of the world. If Ransom were to see her now, would he recognise her?

The thought came out of nowhere, and had invisible fingers tightening around her heart. She had learned the hard way the answer to the question of what became of the broken-hearted. They picked up the pieces and carried on. But they were never the same. Something was irretrievably lost. In her case it was her heart, the greater part of which had gone with him. Having given it, she would never take it back. There would never be another to fill that empty space inside her. She had known she would always love him—and always hate herself for what she had done.

'Not too long now,' Alex said, interrupting her thoughts.

Sam glanced forward. Up ahead of her she could see the turn-off that would take them to the place Alex had grown up in. The house was a rambling affair, with extensions added on in piecemeal fashion as past families had needed room to expand. Consequently the inside was a rabbit warren of stairs and passages, but all adding to its charm. It had countless gables, and several levels of terracing to the rear. Sam adored it.

Beside her Alex flicked the indicator and turned the car onto the road that snaked across the heathland towards the distant coast. There were several more turn-offs before they finally passed through the gates of the small estate. The Hunts were old money. David Hunt had retired to the family home in Norfolk after a long career in banking. Alex was following in his father's footsteps.

'Looks like Karl's down for the weekend,' Alex observed as he caught sight of his older brother standing on the top of the entrance steps. Karl waved, then turned as if someone unseen had spoken to him. 'Things generally liven up when Karl's around.' Sam had met him on a previous visit, and had found him pleasant company.

Alex brought the car to a halt and they climbed out. The sun was almost blinding, and Sam quickly found her sunglasses and slipped them on.

'Now this was definitely worth coming home for. Beautiful blondes with curves in all the right places have long been a penchant of mine,' Karl Hunt teased as he strolled down the steps.

'Not to mention brunettes and redheads,' an amused masculine voice drawled from the shadows of the porticoed entrance.

On hearing it, Sam felt shock go through her from head to toe, and looked round quickly. For an aeon she could swear the earth stopped revolving before lurching on again. She would know that voice anywhere. It was imprinted indelibly on heart and mind. Incredibly, what she had just heard was the voice of Ransom Shaw, yet how could it be? How could it possibly be?

Unaware of her shock, Alex was already starting to laugh as he turned towards the man who now sauntered into view, hands tucked negligently into the pockets of his jeans. He stood at the top of the steps looking at them with a broad grin on his face. Sam could scarcely believe her eyes. Dear God, it *was* Ransom.

The ground moved under her feet for a second, then

stilled. She felt her mouth go dry and then her heart started up a frantic beat. Riveted, she couldn't tear her eyes away from him. Only then did she truly know just how much she had missed him. Seeing him made a light go on inside her, brightening up her world. He was just as she remembered, only more so. His lean yet powerful body was clad in well-worn jeans that hugged his long legs, and a blue chambray shirt with sleeves rolled up above strong forearms, which seemed to strain across his muscled chest.

Sam remembered only too well what it felt like to be held against that perfect body by those two strong arms, and experienced a long-buried curling sensation deep inside herself. Her heart ached with a sudden fierce longing as memories flooded back. The light of love in his eyes. The husky sound of his voice as he told her he loved her. The…

Karl stepped in front of her smiling warmly, blocking out her view. 'Nice to meet you again, Mrs Grimaldi,' he greeted her, offering his hand.

The interruption was like a douche of cold water to Sam. Reality stepped in swift as a sword, cutting off the stream of thoughts. Ransom might still be her one true love, but she had no doubts that it wasn't the same for him. He would hate her now. How could he not, when she had hurt him so badly? Her choice had been bleak, but she had been compelled to take it, for the alternative had been unthinkable.

Sam hastily gathered the remnants of her composure about herself. At the very least she had to look and act calm, even if she wasn't. Her defences had been allowed to go unrepaired with the passing years, so that now they had been breached with remarkable ease. It was painful suddenly seeing him like this, but it never would have been easy. She knew full well what she would see in his eyes when he recognised her, and she must brace herself for it.

Drawing on the *élan* she had learned as the wife of a

wealthy man, Sam whipped off her sunglasses and summoned up a smile for the man before her. 'Call me Sam, please, Karl. How are you?' she responded whilst a bemused Alex moved, walking forward with hand outstretched.

'Well, I'll be damned. Ransom? Great scot, where did you spring from? I haven't seen you in years.'

From her position just a little behind Alex, Sam watched Ransom jog down the steps and take Alex's hand. She had had no idea they knew each other. How on earth could it be?

Sensing her surprise, Karl explained. 'Ransom and I were at university together. Both studying law, and with a love of sailing. He spent a few weeks here one summer, when his parents were abroad. After university, we used to meet occasionally, but then we lost touch. You know how it is. When I bumped into him the other day, I invited him here. Just like old times,' he added happily.

'You must have had a lot of catching up to do,' she responded calmly, knowing it would not be the same for Ransom and herself. She doubted very much if he would want to speak to her.

Karl had more to relate. 'You can say that again. Turns out he has a boat moored just up the coast. He remembered the good times he'd had here and thought he'd try out this neck of the woods again.'

Sam knew it was one of those situations you could never anticipate in a million years. Had she come another weekend, she would never have run into Ransom and discovered he had had a brief acquaintance with Alex's family years ago. Events had conspired to bring them both here now, and it felt as if someone up above was playing a particularly cruel joke.

'I drove up yesterday,' she heard Ransom answer Alex's question.

'Wait a second, didn't I read somewhere that you were out in the South Atlantic wrestling with that American beauty?' Alex declared teasingly, unwittingly sending Sam's stomach plummeting.

She experienced an unexpectedly sharp dart of jealousy at the thought of Ransom with another woman. Silly, really, for the man was not a monk. There would have been others in the last few years. She simply hadn't expected to be reminded of the fact. To imagine him with other women was not the same as knowing it. That was the price of still loving him. She had all of the feelings, with none of the rights.

'She was a beauty, all right. Responded to the lightest of touches. We had a month together, then I had to take her home,' Ransom added with a broad grin, making Alex laugh again.

'Those are the breaks,' Alex commiserated.

The reply made her feel like a fool. It was a short jump to realise he was referring to a boat, not a woman. How could she have forgotten? She had known of Ransom's love of sailing. It appeared his dream of owning his own boat one day had come true. However, she wasn't exactly relieved to feel relief, for it would be better not to feel anything. It would only cause unnecessary pain.

Mentally she grimaced. In an ideal world, maybe, but this was something else. She had been catapulted into a situation she wasn't expecting. Right now she was floundering in a sea of memories, with no life preserver in sight. All she could do was keep herself afloat the best way she could until she was able to make the necessary repairs to her defences.

Not easy with the past so abruptly shunted into the present. Studying the two men as they stood chatting, she could see there was a vibrancy to Ransom that was missing in

Alex, for all his youthful buoyancy. Or perhaps it was just that her vision was being coloured by her emotions.

With their greetings over, Ransom had his first opportunity to take a closer look at Alex's companion, and she braced herself for the blow. What started out as a lazy male inspection soon turned into something altogether different when he recognised her. Blue eyes met grey, and became inextricably locked. Her composure held, but Sam's nerves jolted violently at the power his gaze had to move her still, and at the same time she saw shock fill those dashing grey depths.

It ought to have been no more than that. Shocked recognition should have been followed by a swift recovery for each of them. After all, they had both moved on. Not so. The passing of time had allowed their guard to drop to dangerously low levels. Sam was stunned to discover it was like their first meeting all over again, when out of a clear blue sky something unexpected and purely elemental had passed between them.

It happened now with equal force, revealing the potent attraction they had shared had in no way diminished in the intervening time. The air about them seemed to be positively charged, and in the blink of an eye each knew they were still vitally aware of the other on a physical level. It was a potentially devastating revelation, given their present circumstances. Sam knew she had paled, and she witnessed Ransom's smile fade from his eyes, turning them steely. Both knew they had just reconnected in the most basic way.

For Sam's part it was the very last thing she needed. She had worked so hard to lock her feelings for him away in the recesses of her heart and mind because torturing herself over what might have been was a fruitless exercise. Her feelings for him hadn't and wouldn't change. She loved him. Being aware of him brought to the surface things that were better left buried.

From the tension in his jaw, it was the same for Ransom too. He wouldn't want to feel anything for the woman who had favoured marriage to a wealthy older man over marriage to him.

Oblivious to the undercurrents swirling around them, Alex turned to Sam, saw her shock and mistook the reason for it. 'Hey, it's not what it sounds like. We were talking about boats. Ransom sails boats for a hobby. Races them, too,' he explained.

'He's pretty darn good at it. He'll make the Olympic team one day,' Karl added proudly.

Ransom slipped his hands back into his pockets, producing a smile, though, attuned as she was to his every nuance, Sam could see it didn't touch his mesmerising eyes. 'Knock it off, the pair of you. I'm sure she doesn't want to hear about that.'

Sam knew she had to say something in response, and was so glad she had learned to hold her own in all circumstances. 'I'm afraid I know very little about boats. I've never been on one in my life,' she said politely, with a cool smile of her own, relieved to hear that she sounded calm. Ransom had wanted to take her sailing, but by that time it had been too late.

Alex didn't let her comment pass. 'We can remedy that. You must let Ransom take you out whilst he's here. You'll absolutely love it, I can guarantee that,' he declared enthusiastically.

Sam very nearly groaned aloud. She didn't want to go anywhere with Ransom, least of all on a small boat. 'I'm really not that bothered, Alex. Besides, Karl and his friend might have other plans.' She tried to head Alex off at the pass. Unfortunately, she was about to learn that he didn't give up easily.

Something Ransom was clearly aware of too. 'I'm sure she would rather you went with her,' he demurred at the same time, and his and Sam's gazes locked again long enough for her to see the mockery in his eyes before moving away.

'Don't be daft. I'm no sailor.' Alex rejected that instantly. 'I'm a firm believer in getting the best person for the job, and that's you, Ransom.'

Sam fully expected Ransom to utter a firm refusal, wanting nothing to do with her. However, for a man who had just come face to face with the woman who had made a fool of him, he looked remarkably relaxed. 'I'm sure...?' He glanced at the two men, eyebrows raised, seeking a name, and she knew everybody would be convinced he didn't know her. Which, though it stung, was fine with her, because what they had had was in the past. There was no point in telling anyone what they didn't need to know.

Alex suddenly fell in. 'Sorry, I forgot to introduce you. This is Mrs Samantha Grimaldi, a family friend,' he obliged, turning to smile at her.

'And this handsome devil is my old friend from university, Ransom Shaw,' Karl completed the introduction.

Handsome devil fit the bill all right, for he was handsome, and how well she knew his eyes could hold a devilish gleam. A look like that had set her heart racing and her nerves tingling many a time. That look had led to touching, and recalling her reaction to that made Sam decidedly reluctant to follow up the introduction in the normal way. Good manners, however, left her no choice.

Sam found her heart was thundering like crazy as she reached out to take the hand Ransom offered with a mocking glint in his eye. *Don't react,* she said to herself. *Whatever happens don't react.* Wise advice, for the result was as she had feared. The second their hands touched, it was as if she had been plugged into the mains.

'Pleased to meet you, Mr Shaw,' she managed to say

pleasantly enough. Even maintaining a courteous smile despite the electric sensation that stole her breath away.

Something flashed in those silvery eyes, and his lips twitched as he inclined his head in response. 'Likewise, Mrs Grimaldi.'

As he released her hand his thumb trailed over her palm, and, despite all she did to prevent it, her breath hitched in her throat. Determined not to show how unsettled she was, Sam kept her smile in place. 'Won't you call me Sam, like everyone else?' she invited, rubbing her tingling hand against her thigh surreptitiously.

'Only if you reciprocate and call me by my name,' he rejoined, his gaze daring her to do it. Sam had no intention of backing down.

'Ransom it is, then.'

'And what of Mr Grimaldi? Can we expect him to join you?' Ransom enquired. It sounded like merely polite conversation, but there was a nuance in it that Sam recognised as a charge of her playing away from home. She bristled inwardly but remained calm.

'My husband died six months ago,' she told him stoically, and knew by the glint in his eye that he knew he had struck a nerve by asking about Leno and was pleased.

'That must have been upsetting for you,' he said solicitously, but she knew better than to take his words at face value. He was as good as telling her he didn't believe she was upset at all.

'Leno was a good man. I miss him.' It was true. She had become used to being his wife.

Ransom nodded sombrely. 'I'm sure you were heartbroken to lose him.'

Her stomach twisted as she detected the hard edge to his words. 'We were happy. You must interpret that how you like,' she advised him, looking him squarely in the face, so he would know she was aware of what he was thinking.

She didn't doubt that he believed Leno's fortune had softened the blow.

He smiled faintly. 'I'm sure a beautiful woman such as yourself would know how to treat a man's heart well,' he added ironically, firing off a shot with deadly accuracy.

Sam flinched at the reminder that she hadn't cared about his heart, and took a deep, steadying breath. Raising her chin, she kept smiling. 'I'll take that as a compliment.'

One eyebrow quirked. 'I can assure you it wasn't intended as anything else.'

And the moon is made of green cheese, she thought sardonically. Now, having regained her equilibrium, she took the battle to him. 'What about you, Ransom? Are you happily married?'

'I'm afraid it's going to take a very special woman to make Ransom give up his bachelorhood,' Karl remarked teasingly.

Though it was completely unintentional, those words drove a stake through her heart. Ransom had once told her *she* was special. It had meant everything to her, but she had gone on to prove how unremarkable she was. A thought Ransom echoed.

'They aren't that thick on the ground. Sometimes you think you've found one, but it's all gloss, no substance,' he declared dryly, holding her gaze momentarily.

'I didn't tell you, did I, Alex, that Ransom is listed as one of the top ten most eligible bachelors in this country?' Karl told his brother, hugely amused, and roared with laughter at his friend's sour expression.

'I'm a happily single man,' he pointed out, causing Sam to wince yet again, and Karl wagged a finger in his face.

'Irrelevant. You're available and you're as rich as Croesus. That's all that counts to the women who want to date you.'

Ransom's expression grew ruefully exasperated. 'You

wouldn't find it so funny if you were in my shoes. Since that damn list came out last year, I can't turn around without another would-be Mrs Shaw popping out of the woodwork.'

'Perhaps you should take out a full-page ad in all the papers stating that you are not available,' Alex suggested with a grin.

His brother snorted disparagingly. 'That would never work. Women always believe that they will be the one to change a man's mind.'

Once again Sam winced inwardly. She hadn't needed to change his mind, for they had thought and felt the same way. It was instinctual when you loved someone to want to spend your life with them, and she had been ready for commitment, marriage, the works. Until her brother's actions had changed everything.

'True,' Alex conceded, smiling broadly. 'Sorry, Ransom, but it seems like you're stuck with being one of the country's most sought-after males.'

Sam had never had any trouble picking up Ransom's moods. Right now, though he laughed too, he was far from amused. Well, she wasn't laughing either. She had hurt him enough, and the need to make amends was too strong to fight right then. She had an opportunity and she took it.

'He's right, it isn't funny,' she reproved softly, and drew three pairs of eyes. Two surprised, the other watchful. 'I mean, it must be as awful for a man to know he's only being pursued for his money as it is for a woman to know she's only wanted as a bed mate. It's…demeaning.'

That Ransom didn't believe a word of what she said was in the mocking gleam in his eyes, but he said nothing. Instead, he appeared to take her at face value. 'Why, thank you, Sam. Not many women would be that fair-minded. I doubt, though, that you've ever been demeaned in such a way,' he returned, the rich timbre of his voice sending ripples along her spine, despite the irony she knew to be there. It was a delicious sensation she could definitely have done without under the circumstances.

Sam's smile wavered a fraction as she wondered where he was going with this. 'No, I haven't,' she replied smoothly.

That drew a probing glance from Ransom. 'Of course, it can work the other way too.'

Her thumbs pricked warningly, and she frowned. 'I don't...'

He held her gaze. 'I mean a woman can be pursued for her money, whilst a man can find himself being nothing more than a...bed mate. Equally demeaning, wouldn't you say?' he asked, tipping his head on one side and waiting.

Sam stared back at him, unable to blame him for wanting his pound of flesh. Wounds went deep. How well she knew that. She uttered a tiny wry laugh, then raised her chin a notch and nodded. 'Yes, I would say that was equally demeaning.'

Karl glanced from one to the other and groaned. 'This is getting way too heavy.'

'Let's leave them to it and go get the bags,' Alex declared in disgust, and they both walked over to the car, leaving Sam and Ransom alone.

'What do you know? We have one thing we agree on. Want to try for another?' Ransom asked mockingly and she closed her eyes for an instant.

'Ransom, I...' She had no idea what she was going to say, but wasn't given the chance to find out.

He interrupted her with an equally mocking laugh. 'You know, you didn't have to defend me against the likes of Karl and Alex.'

Sam hastily gathered her thoughts and met his steady look. 'Maybe not, but I've always hated people laughing at another's expense.'

'Karl is an old friend. Friends are put on this earth to rag you,' Ransom pointed out with a shrug.

'But you didn't like it,' she argued, reminding him, should he need reminding, that she had understood him very well once.

'True,' he admitted. 'However, I learned to live with it. You'll have to do the same. As I recall, Alex will remember every silly thing you've ever done and bring it up for his own and others' amusement.'

The comment sent a jolt right through Sam. 'What do you mean by that?'

Ransom shrugged. 'Just giving you a few pointers for when you marry Alex.'

'Marry Alex!' The words spluttered out in the wake of the shock he dealt her. 'Why would you think I was going to marry him?'

'You've got him in your sights, haven't you?' he retorted dryly, and she looked at him, frowning. 'Why else are you here? He's worth a penny or two, and I'm sure you'd agree a woman like you can never have enough money.'

Sam's teeth snapped together as the charge hit home. How dared he? 'For your information, Ransom Shaw, I'm here to see Alex's mother.'

A smile appeared that, despite her anger, hijacked her breath, stealing it away before she could fight off the effect. 'How convenient for you.'

'I am not in love with Alex Hunt,' she countered hardily, so furious she could have slapped Ransom's face for him.

Once again that powerful current flew between them as their gazes touched, but it was in direct counterpoint to what he said next.

'Well, now, darling, we both know *you* don't have to love someone to marry them. All a man needs is the where-withal to keep you in the style you've become accustomed to.'

'You have no right to say that, Ransom,' Sam said with quiet force, although she knew that whatever she said Ransom was going to think the worst. It was her legacy to him. 'I'm not a gold-digger.'

His look was mocking. 'No? Let me see. How could I be convinced of that? I know, I might believe you if you were to deny that money had anything to do with your marriage to Leno Grimaldi,' he declared, pulling the rug out from under her feet. She stared at him, unable to utter the lie.

Ransom laughed mockingly and stepped away just enough to give her breathing room. 'A word of warning, Sam. Don't fall into the trap of thinking you know me. You knew the person I was all those years ago. I'm not that man any more. You'd better walk carefully, and never forget I know what you're capable of.'

Her heart grew heavy at the caution. 'Is that supposed to bother me?'

He smiled faintly. 'I doubt very much if anything could do that. You have nerves of steel. Add that to an avaricious heart, and it makes you a very dangerous woman. Which is why I think we need to have a private talk, you and I,' Ransom declared in a determined voice.

She could see no point to that, and shook her head in swift negation. 'We have nothing to say to each other.'

'I think the situation demands it, don't you?' he argued, with a speaking look.

Sam folded her arms around herself protectively. 'There is no situation, Ransom. You and I are old news.'

'As you say, old news. However, I was thinking about what just happened between us.'

All her nerves jolted at the reminder of that moment when their hands had touched. She ought to have known he would bring it up. 'We connected, but it meant nothing.' She instantly went on the defensive.

'We should at least discuss it,' he insisted.

She laughed incredulously. 'There's no point. A physical reaction means nothing between us.'

'Oh, I got that message the last time,' Ransom drawled derisively. 'You made your feelings very clear then, and I don't have to have it repeated.'

Sam sighed tiredly. 'Then let it go,' she pleaded with him. 'You have to believe me, I'm not interested in Alex. Trust me.'

Her words were met with a look of sheer disbelief. 'Trust you? There are criminals I've helped put in prison I would trust more than you, Sam,' he declared cuttingly, and she was caught on the raw yet again. That was putting her in her place all right. She was now the lowest of the low.

Somehow she managed a shrug. 'OK, then, don't trust me. Just leave me alone.'

No doubt Ransom would have responded to that with something pithy, only the others chose that moment to re-join them. Sam was grateful for the interruption.

'So, how long are you down for, Ransom?' Alex asked as he set their bags down.

'Just the weekend. Karl told your parents he had a surprise for them,' Ransom answered with a wry laugh, and to all intents and purposes their less than friendly conversation had never taken place.

'Naturally, they thought I was bringing a woman,' his friend elaborated. 'Fortunately their disappointment didn't last long when they saw Ransom.'

Reaching out, Ransom hefted the bags Alex had abandoned and started up the steps to the house. 'It's turning out to be one hell of a surprising weekend.'

Only she heard the heavy irony in those last words, and Sam uttered a silent amen to that.

'Why don't you both cut along and say hello to the parents, whilst we take the bags up for you? You'll find them in the garden,' Karl suggested as they reached the bottom of the stairs.

'OK.' Alex nodded. 'Don't forget Sam's using Catherine's old room, Karl.' Catherine was their sister, who had married and left home a few years ago.

Ransom paused in the act of mounting the first stair and glanced back over his shoulder, eyes glittering with amusement. 'Didn't she used to sleep in the old wing?' he wanted to know, whilst looking provocatively at Sam.

Alex nodded. 'You got it. Karl will show you the way.'

Ransom grinned suddenly. 'Good old Mrs H,' he exclaimed, before he turned and carried on up the stairs with Karl.

Sam suspected he was laughing as he went, and she breathed a sigh of relief as he disappeared from view. It felt as if a powerful source of energy had been switched off, allowing her to relax again. These past minutes had been so tense, she felt as if she had run a gruelling race.

Alex led her towards the back of the house and the garden, and she went without protest. Anywhere that Ransom wasn't was a haven right now. Of course, what she really needed was some time alone to get things properly sorted out in her mind. As that wasn't possible, a short breathing space would have to do. At least she would have the opportunity to get her defences propped up before Ransom came back. If their first round was anything to go by, she was going to need nerves of steel for the next.

CHAPTER FOUR

SAM had liked the Hunts from their very first meeting. Working with them on this joint venture was proving to be fun, which was why she looked forward to her visits. Now they greeted her warmly when she and Alex joined them round the table on the lawn.

'It's so lovely to see you again, Sam. Did you meet Ransom yet?' Ellen Hunt enquired of her son, at the same time handing Sam a tall glass of freshly made lemonade in which ice tinkled enticingly.

'We saw him outside with Karl,' Alex informed her as he helped himself to a drink. 'How on earth did you get Karl to abandon his office?' he asked with a grin.

'Your mother threatened him,' David Hunt said teasingly, and received a slap on his arm for his pains.

'As if I would! No, I simply told him it wouldn't do for him to stay shut up in that office all the time,' Ellen Hunt explained to Sam, then grimaced. 'He's turning into a workaholic. Living so far away, we don't see nearly enough of him.'

'You must miss him,' Sam said gently, and the older woman sighed and nodded.

'I miss all the children. This house never seemed so large when we had what seemed like a herd of elephants living here. Now we rattle about in it like a couple of dried up old peas!'

'Call yourself a dried up old pea, but don't include me in that!' her husband protested with a broad wink for Sam, who grinned back.

Ellen Hunt half turned her back on her husband, but there

was a smile in her eyes as she spoke. 'Thankfully Karl had already planned to come and see us, because he planned to surprise us with Ransom. What did you think of him?'

Sam hadn't expected to be put on the spot this way. Having given the impression that she hadn't met him before meant she was compelled to keep up the fiction. 'He seemed...very nice.'

Ellen patted her knee, finding nothing wrong in the remark. 'I thought you'd say that. Everyone likes Ransom,' she pronounced with almost motherly satisfaction. 'He's so handsome and his lifestyle gives him a certain charisma. My boys are handsome too, of course, but working in a bank or boardroom—Karl chose company law—doesn't have the same kind of ring to it, I'm afraid,' she added with an apologetic look at her youngest child.

Alex didn't have an ego problem, and wasn't the least upset. 'Oh, I don't know. I seem to do all right where the ladies are concerned,' he said with a jiggle of his eyebrows, and everyone laughed.

'Have you settled down, now that you've been back in England for a while?' David Hunt addressed himself to Sam. 'How is the job going? Are they keeping you busy at the hotel?'

He was referring to the fact that Sam had had to find somewhere to live on her return to this country. She had also needed to do something with her time. Being financially secure, she had looked for a job where she could be helpful, rather than earn high wages, and was currently employed at one of London's premier hotels, where her skill with languages was in much demand. The situation was ideal, and she enjoyed catering to the needs of the vast range of nationalities staying there.

Sam smiled. 'My apartment is perfect. I'm feeling much more at home, and the view is out of this world. As for the job, the tourists certainly keep me on my toes, David.

Especially at this time of year. I never know what personal disaster I'm going to have to deal with next. But it's fun,' she told him, with a smile that drooped at the edges when she caught sight of Ransom and Karl crossing the lawn towards them. Ransom had an easy grace of movement that still hinted at leashed power. He had always been fit, and she could see that hadn't changed.

'Ah, here are the boys now,' Ellen Hunt announced, following Sam's gaze. Her eyes swept over her son in a motherly fashion. 'Honestly, Karl, those jeans are a positive disgrace!'

'They're comfortable,' he countered, lowering himself to the grass at his mother's feet as all the seats were taken. Ransom stretched out nearby.

'Well, I hope you intend to wear something respectable for the fund-raising dinner, which I expect you to attend, and no arguments,' she told him pointedly, and he grinned at her.

'I promise to wear my best wig and gown for the occasion, though I haven't a clue what you're talking about,' he reassured her lazily, and his mother shook her head helplessly.

'Incorrigible boy! The fund-raiser is for the hospice we're building. Sam represents the Grimaldi Foundation, which is putting up a considerable amount of money. You'll pay for your dinner, and the money raised will be used to help terminally ill children and their families.'

Ransom, who had been observing in silence, now turned to Sam. 'Grimaldi Foundation?' he asked quizzically.

She had been doing her best to avoid looking directly at him, but his question forced her to glance his way. After their initial meeting, she wasn't surprised to feel her heart skip a beat at the sheer male beauty of him. She would have given a lot not to be susceptible to his brand of sexual magnetism, but some things just were—would always be.

Doing her best to ignore her senses, she had to admire the way he appeared relaxed and completely at ease. Clearly he intended to act as if nothing unexpected had happened. Sam knew it made good sense to do the same.

'I set it up in my husband's name. This is just the beginning,' she returned lightly, glancing at Ellen and smiling. 'Who knows? We might have further projects in the future,' she added, and the older woman nodded enthusiastically.

'Have you decided if you're going to invite your family to the dinner yet, Sam?' David Hunt put in. They had been discussing the function for some weeks now.

'My parents will come, I hope, but the others are pretty scattered,' she told him. 'Tony is the farthest away, in Australia,' she added with a rueful shrug. She had never heard from him, but her parents had told her he was doing well.

'Where have you been living, Sam? Something tells me you didn't get that tan in England,' Ransom queried, and his friend tutted.

'Take it easy, Ransom, you're not in the courtroom now. Don't bark questions at the poor woman.'

Seeing him being taken to task, Sam was tempted to laugh, but bit her lip to hold it back as Ransom sighed long-sufferingly. 'It was a reasonable question, and I did not bark. I never bark.'

'You do! I've heard you!' Karl contradicted him immediately.

'I lived in Italy until my husband died,' Sam explained quickly, bringing the friendly exchange of words to an end.

'Sam has a holiday home overlooking the Adriatic,' Ellen Hunt added, but she didn't see the glint of mockery that produced in Ransom's eyes. Sam did and heartily wished the remark unsaid.

'How the rich live!' He sighed, shaking his head, and again Karl took up the cudgels.

'You're a fine one to talk! You own an ocean-going yacht, a house in the best part of London and an apartment in New York. Not to mention that little place on Corfu!'

Ransom merely grinned. 'I earned all that with the sweat of my brow,' he retorted, and Sam felt the true sting behind the words. She had married money, making her morals clearly less than pure.

'Whilst I inherited mine. I'm sorry if that offends you,' she told him in a cool, calm voice that nonetheless dared him to say more at his peril.

He looked her in the eye, smiling with lazy charm. 'Inherited money doesn't offend me, Sam. I'm sure you loved your husband.'

Oh, but he was clever. To anyone listening he sounded so sincere. She, on the other hand, knew differently. He was openly doubting her feelings, and she had to counter it immediately. Which she did by holding his gaze.

'I'm sure you can understand that my feelings for my husband are private.'

Ransom inclined his head without releasing her eyes. 'I understand perfectly,' he confirmed, and once again only she knew he was referring to her so-called gold-digging habits, not her state of mourning.

'How come you married an Italian? Did you meet him on holiday?' Alex asked with idle curiosity.

Sam was glad of the diversion. At least she could look at someone else for a while. 'No. I knew him through my family. I'm a quarter Italian myself.'

'That's very interesting.' Ransom's smooth tones entered the conversation, much to Sam's chagrin. 'I've always considered them a passionate people. Strong in love and hate. Wholly committed to their families. Hurt one and you hurt them all. Is that how it is with you?' he asked Sam, who could scarcely avoid answering, though she would have liked to.

'Oh, yes. There's nothing I wouldn't do to help my family if they were in trouble,' Sam said honestly. It was, after all, something she had firsthand experience of.

Ransom tipped his head questioningly. 'Nothing you wouldn't do? That's rather a rash statement, wouldn't you say?'

She stared at him, seeing the insolence deep in his eyes. 'I would stop short at anything illegal.'

He smiled. 'Yet some things are criminal without being illegal. Crimes of the heart, for instance.'

It was a low blow, but she smiled back, equally coolly. 'Surely that would depend on your point of view.'

'Hey!' Alex broke in at that point, much to Sam's relief. 'Are you still giving her the third degree?'

Ransom shrugged easily. 'Just making idle conversation.'

'If that was idle, I'd say you've spent too much time in the courtroom,' Alex upbraided him, but that only had Ransom regarding her with a subtler form of mockery.

'Did I upset you? I apologise if I did.'

'There's no need. I grew up in a household where we children were subjected to far more searching questions. Especially if we were late getting home from a date. If I could survive that, I can survive anything,' Sam responded with wry humour.

'Let's not get started on over-protective parents. I could give you chapter and verse!' Ellen Hunt declared with a roll of her eyes. 'Now then, Sam. Shall we pop along to the study and have a look at the plans and arrangements now? It would leave the weekend free for us to enjoy your company.'

Sam jumped at the opportunity to put distance between herself and Ransom. 'That sounds like a wonderful idea,

Ellen,' she responded with a smile. Rising, she joined the other woman by the table.

'We'll leave you men in peace for a while,' Ellen declared with an impish grin.

Out of the corner of her eye, Sam could see Ransom lying stretched out on the grass. He might look relaxed, but she knew better than anyone that it was all an act. Only a fool would imagine that he was happy about the situation, and she was no fool. He would want that talk, but she had no intention of obliging him. There was going to be a battle of wills going on this weekend, combined with a great deal of emotional stress. Something told her it was going to be a long two days.

When Sam eventually went upstairs to freshen up before dinner that evening, she was wound up tighter than a drum. She had spent an interesting few hours with Ellen, talking over the plans for the hospice and the ways of raising yet more funds for it. Yet for all that she felt as if she were playing a part. She was doing her best to act naturally, but, as more time passed, the more *unnatural* she felt.

Sensing the beginnings of a tension headache, she took a couple of painkillers and propped herself up against the pillows on the bed, hoping to ease away some of the tension before she had to go down and face Ransom again. However, the second she began to relax, memories started resurfacing, tumbling into her mind like pennies from a slot machine. They were inevitably accompanied by a flood of emotions. There was no forgetting the intense happiness she had felt, knowing how much she loved Ransom, nor the soul-destroying anguish when she had brought it to an end.

She had loved beyond reason, beyond hope. There *was* no hope for a future with him in it. The truth was she hadn't expected to be free so soon, and that left her in an emotional vacuum where it was impossible to go back or forwards. There was only the now, with painful memories surfacing at every turn. She had locked her heart away in an icy cavern, but seeing Ransom had created devastating cracks in its walls, and they were melting, leaving her open to all the old pain and vulnerable to the new.

It had been such a tremendous shock to discover Ransom here, but it didn't change anything. He might have loved her once, but that was ancient history. They had had something special, but she had been forced to treat it like dross. Nothing could put that right.

So here they were, caught up in the unexpected drama of an old relationship, where all that remained on his part was his hatred of her for what she had done, and her undying love for him.

No, that wasn't quite correct. There was also the little matter of the resurgence of their mutual attraction. She really hadn't expected that. With their affair over, she had believed that attraction had shrivelled and died. Now she realised it had merely been dormant, and had stirred to life in an instant. She could have done without it bringing its particular brand of havoc to her ordered life, for it was going to be a painful reminder of how things had been and how they never would be again.

She had no doubts the powerful sensual pull would be as unwelcome to Ransom as it was to her, though their reasons differed. He would have no desire to act upon it, and every intention of ignoring it. She was going to do the same. When he had walked out of her life, she had known he would not be walking back into it. Years had gone by, but he had forgotten nothing. Forgiven nothing.

Her priority now must be to get through the next two days, and then they wouldn't meet again. After the weekend they would be getting on with their own lives. Out of sight was out of mind, and, however strong the connection might still be, it would fade away again. Besides, she had discovered unknown strengths in the years of her marriage, and she knew she could cope with meeting Ransom just this once.

Sighing, she glanced at her watch, realised how late it was getting and scrambled off the bed. Walking into the *en suite* bathroom, she washed her face and reapplied her make-up. One thing she knew for certain: life went on regardless of old wounds. So she would make herself look presentable and go back downstairs, and not for an instant would she show that all was not as it should be.

Dinner that evening turned out to be an entertaining if poignant affair. As this visit was the first in many years, Ransom was called upon to relate some of the bizarre things that happened in the courtroom, and did so with the droll sense of humour she had known so well. It was impossible not to remember that he had always been able to make her laugh, and, despite her best intentions, there was no way she could stop her heart from twisting wryly.

It would have been so much easier had she been able to dislike everything about him, but that just was not possible. Her beleaguered heart had no defences against him. He was still the man she had fallen in love with.

Despite her very real anguish, she was still able to laugh with the rest of them. And when her eye was caught by the twinkle in his, or the dimple that appeared in his cheek whenever he was secretly amused at something one of the others said, she took a deep breath and told herself it would all be over soon. She would be able to retreat to her room and indulge in a good cry in only a few hours. She could hold out till then.

They took coffee in the lounge, and had just finished when Ransom was called away to answer a telephone call.

'I hope you don't mind, Mrs H. I left this number should something important come in about a case,' he apologised for the interruption before striding off to the study to take it.

Whilst he was gone, Ellen Hunt produced a collection of photograph albums and insisted Sam sit beside her whilst she went through them. Much to Alex's and Karl's embarrassment. Sam grinned at their pained expressions whenever their mother declared what lovely babies they had been.

'Don't you dare show her any of me in the buff!' Alex commanded vainly, knowing his mother too well to expect her not to do that very thing.

'But you look so cute on that velvet cushion,' Karl teased, laughing out loud when his brother groaned.

'Is somebody being murdered?' Ransom asked as he sauntered back into the room.

Much to Sam's dismay, Ellen waved him over. 'Oh, you must come and look at this photo, Ransom,' she invited.

'Don't you dare!' Alex wailed, but Ransom merely grinned his roguish grin and went to stand behind the settee, looking over Ellen Hunt's shoulder. 'Oh, hell,' Alex groaned, collapsing back into his chair at the futility of attempting to stop his mother when she was in full flood.

David Hunt held out a glass to each of his sons. 'Have some brandy and keep a stiff upper lip. This is just one of the crosses we men have to bear.'

'Bare being the operative word,' Ransom quipped, taking devilish delight in the younger men's discomfiture.

Sam's laughter faded, for she was vibrantly aware of him leaning on the back of the settee. She could feel the faint brush of his breath in her hair as he breathed, and smell the subtle trace of the male cologne he had used when he shaved. It was cool, not too spicy, and reminded her all too clearly of long, passion-filled nights spent in his arms. Hastily she shut down that line of thought, and willed it to remain closed.

'Oh, now, this is the only one we have of you and Karl, Ransom,' Ellen declared, pointing to the picture of two young men on the beach, digging with spades, and wearing handkerchiefs knotted at the corners to make hats. 'You'd never think they were studying law, would you?' She invited Sam's closer inspection.

Sam's natural curiosity overcame her reluctance and she edged closer to examine the photo. She could definitely see the grown man in the younger version. He didn't have the physique she remembered, but that grin was still the same. She found herself smiling at the reminder of happier days.

'What were you building? A sandcastle?' she asked him impudently, tipping her head up and round and finding herself virtually nose to nose with him as he bent down to get a better look.

Dancing grey eyes laughed into blue, stealing her breath away. 'A boat, of course!' he returned smartly.

Swallowing hard, Sam concentrated on the photo, but it was no longer easy when it seemed as if every nerve in her body was attuned to his presence. Ellen chatted away, turning the pages, seemingly not bothered that Sam had fallen silent.

'And this is when Karl won his first trophy,' Ellen declared proudly. 'What was the name of that young man who partnered you? Ransom had hurt himself, so someone else stepped in. Tim? Tom…?' she asked, and Ransom reached down between her and Sam to adjust the page.

As he did so the back of his hand brushed across Sam's cheek. It was like a lick of flame, and there was no way she could stop herself from breathing in sharply as the heat of it radiated through her system. Feeling sure she must have been heard, she glanced around the room, but nobody was looking her way. She was on the point of being relieved when she discovered there was one person who had noticed.

'Sorry, did my ring catch you?' Ransom enquired solicitously, yet when she was compelled by good manners to look at him his eyes were alight with mockery.

'No. I'm fine,' she denied, realising with a tiny jolt that the action had been deliberate. For reasons of his own he had wanted to check out her reaction, and she had betrayed herself with that sharp intake of breath.

She tuned out, mind spinning. This simply had to stop happening. Wasn't there a law that said you couldn't respond where you were no longer loved? If not, there should be. By rights she should be feeling nothing, and yet her skin still tingled, although it had been the merest touch. It was bordering on recklessness to still be so attuned to him. Hadn't she sent the man out of her life six years ago, and moved on? Shouldn't her senses be switched off where he was concerned, not working overtime? Why...?

Suddenly she became aware of an expectant hush, and glanced up swiftly, discovering that this time she *was* being stared at. Faint colour washed up into her cheeks. 'Sorry, did somebody say something?'

Alex grinned at her. 'You mean you didn't see the herd of wildebeest which charged through a moment ago?'

Recovering, Sam wagged an admonitory finger at him. 'Don't exaggerate, there were only half a dozen!'

'What number constitutes a herd?' Ransom enquired mockingly as he straightened up, finally making it possible for Sam to breathe freely once more.

Karl immediately took up the debate, and his father joined in. Having started the ball rolling, Ransom left them to it, and Sam watched him cross to the cocktail trolley and pour himself a drink, which he downed in one go, as if he had really needed it. Which intriguingly suggested he had been affected by the brief contact he had instigated. How fascinating! Not that she actively wanted proof of their mutual awareness. However, knowing how Ransom felt towards her, she was made to feel better somehow by the fact that he was unsettled too.

Ransom didn't return to the settee after he set his glass aside, but took up a station by the fireplace, one arm resting negligently along the mantelpiece. Sam simply couldn't seem to resist looking at him. Though she knew it was crazy, time and again she found her gaze being drawn in his direction, even when he wasn't speaking. She couldn't help recalling that deliberate touch on her cheek. Why had he done it? What was he up to?

She was no nearer knowing the answers when she retired for the night some hours later. Closing the bedroom door, she slumped back against it. She felt totally and utterly drained. Being so aware of one person and doing her best not to show it was proving to be an unbelievable strain. If she had had a good reason to cut the visit short, she would probably have used it, but she didn't have one. The sensible thing to do was avoid Ransom as much as possible. Maybe then she would be able to relax.

Pushing herself away from the door, she headed for the bathroom. Perhaps Ransom would decide to leave, she mused wistfully, then immediately experienced a sinking feeling in her stomach. Illogical as it was, deep down inside she didn't want him to go. Not now that she had seen him again. Her brain might say cut it short, but her heart wanted more. It wasn't a good position to be in, but she would just have to grit her teeth and see it through. Now, if she could just get some sleep she might be in a state to cope with whatever was coming her way...

Several hours later, Sam set the milky saucepan in the sink and ran water into it. The clock on the kitchen wall showed quarter past two in the morning, and she sighed heavily, picking up her mug of chocolate and carrying it to the table. So much for sleep, she thought wryly as she made herself comfortable, propping her bare feet on the stretcher of the next chair.

She had tossed and turned for hours, her brain too active to allow her tired body to get the sleep it needed. Her last resort had been a mug of hot, milky chocolate, and she had slipped on a scarlet silk robe over its matching nightdress and made her way down to the kitchen. At least making the drink had given her thoughts a different path to follow for a while.

A creaking sound from beyond the kitchen caused her to freeze and look round at the door, ears straining to pick up further sounds. She had been careful not to make any noise and disturb the family on her way downstairs. However, there was no other sound, and she relaxed, accepting that it was simply the old house settling.

Sipping carefully at the steaming liquid, Sam let out another ragged sigh. It was Ransom who had kept her awake, but there was no prize for knowing that. Memories were haunting her, playing over and over. She dragged a hand through her hair, tousling it as she had countless times these past few hours.

Uppermost had been recalling just how cruel she had been. She had severed the connection with icy deliberation, knowing she was breaking his heart. It had been callous and cruel, and she hated herself for it to this day. Even though Ransom had later discovered she was marrying Leno, the things he had accused her of hadn't helped to lighten the burden of guilt. She needed to be forgiven, but knew she never would be.

That should have been the end of the story, but life threw in another of its twists. Here she was in the same house as Ransom, and as aware of him as if the past six years had never happened. She hadn't expected that. Hadn't expected to ever see him again. She had made a point of avoiding their old haunts on her return to England. Knowing the hopelessness of the situation, she would have hoped to feel nothing, but heart and mind were travelling different paths.

She knew now, as she had then, that she would never be indifferent to Ransom, no matter what happened. He had her heart, and would have till the day she died. It was a sobering thought.

Just then the unmistakable click of the door opening brought her head shooting round, and her heart gave an almighty jolt in her chest as Ransom entered the room and closed the door behind him, leaning back against it to eye her consideringly. He was dressed in his jeans, but that was all. Even his feet were bare. He made an impressive sight, and her senses were overwhelmingly impressed. Immediately the room seemed to shrink, until the world was no bigger than the space between them.

Sam sat up straighter, all semblance of relaxing gone. 'What are you doing here?'

'I've come for our cosy little chat,' he informed her mildly. 'Everyone's asleep, so we're unlikely to be disturbed.'

That was what he thought! She was already disturbed just by his being here! 'I told you there's nothing to say,' she reminded him, then frowned as something struck her about his unexpected arrival. 'Just a second. How did you know I was here?'

That brought a faintly insolent smile to his lips. 'I heard you go downstairs, so I followed you,' he explained, crossing his arms and looking prepared to stay awhile. The action enhanced powerful muscles and was not lost on her. Consequently it took several seconds for his words to register.

'Heard me?' That startled her, for she knew she had been at pains to be quiet.

'Not a hard thing to do when I have the room next to

yours,' he explained with more than a hint of sardonic amusement at her reaction.

Sam's heart skipped a beat and her eyes widened in surprise. 'The next room?' That was totally unexpected. She had believed she was alone in that part of the house. It gave her an unsettling feeling knowing Ransom was so close.

A taunting smile curved his lips. 'Working out the possibilities? Don't worry, I shan't be paying you a visit.'

That was calculated to put her back up, and it did so instantly. 'I wouldn't want you to!'

His smile grew more wolfish. 'Yet you're still attracted to me.'

The blunt statement took her breath away, because it was true and they both knew it. Ransom took advantage of her momentary silence to continue.

'Is that why you tossed and turned so much? Because you had an itch you couldn't scratch?' he insinuated mockingly, and Sam's jaw very nearly fell off, she was so surprised by the charge.

Consequently she jackknifed to her feet in outrage. 'How dare you?'

Ransom pushed himself away from the door and took a step towards the table. 'Keep your voice down, Sam, unless you want an audience,' he cautioned levelly. Hooking out a chair, he sat down facing her. 'That's a very tantalising little number you're wearing. If memory serves me right, the only thing you looked better in than silk was nothing at all,' he added provocatively, and she felt the brush of his gaze like a lick of flame as he ran it over her.

Her senses, which had barely settled down, were kick-started into wakefulness, and all the fine hairs on her body abruptly stood to attention. She hadn't expected him to say something so provocative, and her defences were breached. Her eyes automatically went to his tanned chest, and the urge to reach out and touch was so strong she almost groaned aloud. Damn it, he was far too sexy for sanity. The sensible part of her wished he'd put something on, whilst the other revelled in the nearness of so much bare flesh.

Belatedly it dawned on her that she was positively eating him with her eyes, and rather hastily she averted her gaze. 'Cut it out, Ransom. You didn't come here to flirt with the enemy.'

He laughed huskily, sounding genuinely amused. 'Is that how you see yourself? Interesting.'

Her temper rose. He was playing cat and mouse with her as if she were a witness in the box, and she most definitely did not like it. 'Get to the point, damn it,' she snapped, then groaned inwardly because she knew it was in her own best interests to remain calm and in control.

Ransom laughed again. 'Are you going to sit down, or is it your intention to give me a perfect view of your navel?'

Sam was sorely tempted to hit him, but slowly sank back onto her seat instead.

'That's better, isn't it?' he pronounced aggravatingly, but she held her tongue. 'You're looking good, Sam. What a difference six years and unlimited money can make. You left England with nothing, and return a wealthy widow. Nice work.'

Only Ransom could reduce her marriage to three blistering sentences. 'I took my marriage seriously,' she stated shortly, not wanting to have this conversation, but caught up in it anyway. If she had given it more thought, she would have known it was inevitable. He was not going to be diverted.

Ransom's lips twitched derisively. 'Of course you did. The very last thing you would have wanted was for the old guy to divorce you. But I'm intrigued. How can you profess to miss your husband, when mere hours ago you responded to me?'

She had the perfect answer to that, but it was one she could never tell him. Instead she went for the obvious. 'You don't have to love someone to respond to them.'

Now that brought a steely glint to his eye. 'So I discovered firsthand six years ago. You were adamant it was just sex for you then. Or are you going to tell me you've changed your mind and it was love after all?'

A shaft of pain speared her heart, where all her love for him was locked away. 'Why would I do that?' she asked, not yet understanding where this was going.

His lips twitched. 'It occurred to me that after you heard that I was a very eligible bachelor, you might have reconsidered your options. After all, a woman like you would be bound to keep her eye on the main chance.'

Now she understood. He thought that she might be turning her attention to him, now that she knew he was richer than Alex. That he could think so contemptuously of her was a killer blow, and she struggled to respond calmly. 'Do you really think I would waste my time that way?' she charged him with some mockery of her own. 'It's clear how you feel. You hate me.'

To her surprise he found that highly amusing. 'Hate you? Oh, no, darling, I went through hating you a long time ago. Now I rarely think about you.'

That stung, and she responded instinctively. Her eyebrows arched delicately as she regarded him with disdain. 'And yet *you're* still attracted to *me*.'

Had she hoped to unsettle him, she failed miserably. Ransom merely inclined his head in wry acknowledgement. 'That came as a surprise to me, too. I thought, feeling as I had about you, that that powerful connection would be gone. However, I'm not in the market for a wife. Even one as beautiful and wealthy as you.'

Sam looked him squarely in the eye. 'Good, because I've told you I'm not looking for a replacement for Leno, either.'

That sardonic smile returned to his lips. 'Forgive me if I have trouble believing you. I know you too well. You're a dab hand at flattering to deceive. You'll say anything to get what you want.'

'I never promised you anything, Ransom,' she insisted quietly, and he smiled a smile that failed to reach his eyes.

'No, you didn't. You merely lied.'

Sam's gaze dropped to the cooling mug of chocolate, so she didn't see the inscrutable expression that momentarily spread across his face. Yes, she had lied, but not in the way he thought. She sighed. 'Look, this is getting us nowhere. I'm sorry I hurt you, but that's in the past.' She raised her eyes to his. 'Isn't it?'

'It isn't your past that bothers me, but your present plans.'

Her eyes flashed out her annoyance and she momentarily lost her cool again. 'How many times do I have to tell you? I don't have any plans!'

'Until I'm convinced,' he rejoined hardily.

Sam pushed herself back in her seat, arms folded to hide the fact her hands were trembling with suppressed emotions. 'I've said I'm sorry. I've told you neither you nor Alex are in any danger from me. If you don't believe me, there's nothing else I can do.'

His expression became assessing as he looked at her, head tipped to one side. 'You could leave,' he said softly, and suddenly she was filled with anger.

'I'm damned if I will! I have business here. If you don't like my being in the same house as you, you go!'

Ransom immediately shook his head. 'And leave the field open to you? I think not. Who knows what you could get up to, given a free rein?'

'Dear God, but you have some nerve!' she gasped, anger being swamped by dismay that clogged her throat. 'I'm not a gold-digger and you know it.'

At that his expression became distant and he shook his head. 'Did I ever know you, Sam? Seems to me you're capable of anything.'

Tears stung the backs of her eyes, but she refused to allow them to fall. 'Then you had a lucky escape, didn't you?'

'I've seen it that way for a long time,' he confirmed calmly, totally in control of the situation.

Sam struggled to keep her emotions from showing, though her stomach was churning wildly. 'So, what happens now?'

Ransom regarded her steadily for a nerve-tearing age before answering. 'Nothing, provided you steer clear of any entanglement with Alex. If anything happens to the contrary, then I shall be obliged to tell him what I know.'

She glared at him, not alarmed by the threat, yet hurt that he would make it. 'Don't they call that blackmail?'

He grinned back. 'Some might. I call it being sensible. So, what's your answer?'

Sam gave him the answer he wanted. It made no difference to her, as she had no plans to do what he was thinking anyway. 'I accept.'

His smile was tinged with mockery. 'Thought you might. Afraid of what I might say?'

This mockery was something he had never directed against her before, and she found it hurtful. But then, he probably wanted to hurt her—assuming he thought she could be hurt. All she could do was counter-attack.

'Actually, you're one of the few people I would trust to tell the truth.'

'Shame I can't say the same about you, darling,' he returned, and the meaningless endearment stung.

'Stop calling me that. I'm not your darling any more,' she snapped.

'Sorry,' he apologised with patent insincerity as he got up. 'Old habits die hard.'

She stared at him in frustration. 'Are you enjoying seeing me squirm?'

He grinned broadly. 'Having the boot on the other foot has its amusing side.'

Sam rose swiftly and took her mug over to the sink, tossing the contents down the drain. 'It never occurs to you that you might be wrong, does it?' she remarked scornfully, rinsing the mug under the hot tap before putting it in the dishwasher. With nothing left to do, she turned to face him again, leaning against the unit as she waited for his answer.

'On the contrary, I often have doubts, but not about you. On that subject I'm perfectly clear,' he told her sardonically. With that he walked over to the door, pausing before opening it to look back at her. 'I'd say it was a pleasure seeing you again, darling, but we both know I'd be lying. Oh, and try not to make too much noise on your way back to bed.'

A faintly mocking smile hovered around his mouth as he nodded and left the room. Sam closed her eyes, sagging back against the sink as the tension slowly drained away. Sadness crept over her at how changed Ransom was. She knew she was responsible for a lot of it, and she wasn't proud of herself. She could only remind herself that she had wanted him to stop loving her, and had succeeded. She would just have to bear the fruits of her success with as little outward show of pain as possible.

She started to laugh, though her eyes glittered moistly. Lord, this was going to be more of a punishment than she had ever thought possible. Her own sense of guilt had demanded that she should pay for what she had done, but she would never have thought of this. She brushed away a tear and straightened up. She could take it. After all, she'd already done the hardest thing—giving him up. Anything else was small potatoes by comparison.

Crossing to the door, she looked round to make sure she had left everything tidy.

Ransom was barking up the wrong tree, but, as she couldn't convince him otherwise, she had to let him get on with it. She knew what she was here for, and that was all that mattered. She had to stop reacting so emotionally to the things he said. Nothing would be gained by letting him continue to upset her, even if he didn't know his barbs were striking home.

Sleep seemed as far away as ever, and she knew she was in for a long night. Sighing, Sam switched off the light and quietly let herself out.

CHAPTER FIVE

SATURDAY morning brought with it bright sunshine, her-alding the start of a glorious day. However, as chirpy as the birds in the garden might be, after the restless night she had had, Sam was a long way from firing on all cylinders. A shower went some way to waking up her sluggish brain, but she knew she was in no way ready for the day ahead.

Dressing in designer jeans and a strappy silk top, she went down to breakfast with a fluttery stomach. Of course, as luck would have it, the first person she saw when she entered the breakfast room was Ransom standing at the sideboard. He, too, was wearing jeans again, and his bril-liantly white tee shirt fitted him so well, he could just as easily not have been wearing it.

Whilst her senses were registering the attraction, her heart was registering pleasure. She couldn't help it, and she knew it would only make things harder for herself, but, after so long a time apart, deep down she was happy to see Ransom. At moments like these, it didn't matter what he thought of her. Her heart knew a long-forgotten joy at his presence.

'Morning, sleepyhead,' Alex greeted her cheekily from the breakfast table, and she glanced round, finally noting that the other members of the family were there too.

Producing a smile in response to the grin he was wearing, she went to join them. 'Good morning. Sorry to be so late,' she apologised to Ellen Hunt, who waved it away with a smile.

'There's a rule in this house—nobody can be late for

breakfast at the weekend. Now, there's plenty of food left, so help yourself, dear.'

Which, of course, gave Sam no option but to go and join Ransom. He was chewing on a crispy slice of bacon he had filched from one of the dishes, and turned, resting a hip against the sideboard to give her room.

'Sleep well?' he enquired conversationally, but a quick glance at his eyes noted the mocking insolence there.

'Perfectly, thank you,' she returned politely. She reached for the lid of a silver serving dish at the same time as Ransom did. Their hands touched, and an electric charge ran up her arm, causing her to gasp and let go. The resultant crash echoed round the room, making her wince and bringing hot colour to her cheeks. 'Sorry!' she apologised to the room at large.

'For the sake of the Hunt family silver, allow me,' Ransom quipped, gallantly removing the lid and holding it so she could see the bacon and sausages set out beneath it. 'You seem a little jittery this morning,' he added in a barely audible undertone.

Reaching for a plate and a server with hands that carried a faint tremble, she helped herself to some of each. 'Go away!' she snapped at him under her breath as she did so.

'Don't you think it would look a bit obvious if I left the room the instant you entered it?' he responded mockingly, helping himself to another slice of bacon before setting down the lid. He raised another helpfully. 'Scrambled egg?'

She was momentarily tempted to decorate his face with it, but thought better of it just in time. 'OK, don't leave, just go and sit at the table like a normal person!' she suggested, helping herself to a little of the fluffy egg.

Ransom moved along, but didn't leave. 'Toast and butter?' Holding the bacon between his teeth, he held up the toast rack and dish of beautifully curled butter. She nearly dropped the toast as she snatched a slice. 'Am I making you nervous?' he wanted to know next, polishing off the bacon and wiping his hands on a napkin.

Was he making her nervous? Sam took a deep breath and glared at him. 'You're looking death in the face!' she snapped with a sweet smile and gritted teeth.

A response that merely caused him to grin broadly. 'Go and sit down and I'll pour you some coffee. The way you're acting, you'll probably scald yourself with it.'

He was probably right. She was a bit too dithery for safety, but the coffee would help with that. She hoped. Never one to look a gift-horse in the mouth, she took the opportunity to move away. When she looked at her plate after she sat down, she didn't think she could eat any of it, her stomach was churning so, but she made the effort. It was delicious, and after a bite or two her appetite was swiftly resurrected. Thankfully, after Ransom set a cup of coffee beside her, he returned to the sideboard, giving her room to breathe and in the end she cleared her plate to the last crumb.

'What are you going to do today?' Ellen Hunt asked her sons as they all sat drinking coffee. 'Have you made any plans?'

'Ransom is going to take Sam sailing,' Alex pronounced, as if it had all been decided, causing Sam's eyes to widen in surprise.

'What a good idea. As we finished our business yesterday, the time is your own,' the older woman responded cheerfully before Sam could say a word in denial. 'Ransom is the best.'

'I'm sure he is,' Sam managed to put in swiftly, before anyone else spoke. 'However, I thought it was just a suggestion.' she said, looking pointedly at Alex who, much to her irritation, grinned back as if it were a great joke.

Ellen, meanwhile, had misunderstood her argument.

'There's nothing to be worried about. Ransom is quite safe.'

Receiving no help from any quarter, Sam could feel the trap closing around her and smiled wanly. 'I wouldn't doubt it for a second, but has anyone asked Ransom what he wants to do? Maybe he and Karl have other plans.' She laid more than a little stress on those last words as she turned her attention to Ransom. That he registered them was in the twitching of his lips.

To her dismay, Ellen laughed. 'Of course he wouldn't mind taking you along.'

'I'd offer,' Karl put in from his seat at the end of the table. 'Unfortunately I have a meeting this morning at the yacht club.'

To Sam's consternation, Ransom didn't look in the least put out, but accepted his fate by crossing to the older woman and bending to kiss her cheek. 'Of course I don't mind, Ellen. I'll take Sam with me, if that's what she wants.' He neatly returned the ball back to her court.

She really wouldn't have minded causing a spot of mayhem right then. Of course it wasn't what she wanted, but she had been backed into a corner, and there was little she could do but give in gracefully. 'OK, sailing it is, then,' she declared brightly, whilst her heart sank.

Though he smiled back at her, she couldn't imagine Ransom wanted her on his boat any more than she wanted to be there. Well, in all honesty, most of her didn't want to be there, but there was a tiny part way deep inside that saw the trip as an unexpected chance to be alone with him again. How insane was that?

'I'll go and check on the tide and the weather. Then I'd better clean out the Land Rover. I wouldn't want you to mess up your clothes,' Ransom declared. He caught Sam by the shoulder, unwittingly sending heat radiating through her from his touch. 'Make sure you have a change of clothes and something warm to put on. I'll meet you outside in, say, half an hour.'

Sam cleared a frog from her throat. 'Thirty minutes. Yes, OK,' she agreed huskily.

As the younger man left the room David Hunt rose from his seat. 'We'll have to be making a move, too. Ellen wants to go into Norwich for some shopping.'

'We were going to invite you to join us, Sam, but you'll have much more fun with Ransom,' his wife added with an impish smile.

'We'll have lunch out, so we won't see you until later. Have fun, and don't do anything silly like drowning yourself,' David teased before shepherding his wife through the door.

When they had gone, Sam flexed her shoulder where she could still feel the imprint of Ransom's hand like a brand. He had always had magic in his fingers, and clearly that hadn't changed. Neither had her susceptibility. Pushing her cup away, she looked at Alex, who had got her into this.

'I wish you hadn't done that,' she declared, expression rueful.

He looked rather crestfallen at her complaint. 'I thought it would be fun for you,' he argued, making her wince and shake her head.

'Oh, Alex, I'm the last person Ransom wants on his boat with him,' she exclaimed wryly, and he frowned heavily.

'Why on earth would you say that?' His surprise was tangible.

Sighing, she dragged a hand through her hair. 'Well, you did rather put him in a position where he couldn't say no.'

Alex pooh-poohed that immediately. 'Trust me, no man would turn down the opportunity of having a beautiful woman alone on a boat with him!' he told her with a grin.

Sam couldn't help but laugh. 'Thanks for the compliment. Let's hope Ransom doesn't mind the fact that I know nothing about boats.'

'You'll be fine. Believe me, there's nobody better to teach you,' he added for good measure.

Sam winced, then sighed. 'Hopefully we'll get through the day without him murdering me,' she declared as she headed for the door. 'What are you going to be doing whilst I'm out there having all this fun?'

'Oh, I'll probably look up some old friends. Go for a drink. Boy stuff.'

'OK, well, don't drink too much. And spare me a thought from time to time.'

'Have fun!' he called after her, voice ringing with laughter.

Sam, however, felt her smile slipping away as she went up to her room to throw a few things together. It felt as if she were going to her own execution—which was rather extreme. On the other hand, how more alone with him could she be than on a boat in the middle of the North Sea? Wasn't that a recipe for disaster? However, she couldn't back out now, so all she could do was grit her teeth and hope for the best.

When she walked outside some ten minutes later, she found Ransom and Alex chatting by a much-used Land Rover. Both men turned to face her, and she could tell from the glint in Ransom's eye and the smile on Alex's face that they had been talking about her. Now what? she wondered.

'Ready?' Ransom checked, and she nodded.

'As I'll ever be.' If she had to do this, then the sooner they began, the sooner they finished.

Alex helped her into her seat, then gave her the thumbs-up as the car moved off.

'I thought you might have changed your mind,' Ransom remarked dryly once they were on their way, and Alex was a dwindling figure in the rear window.

Sam kept her gaze firmly fixed on the passing countryside. 'I was tempted.'

The instant the doors had closed them in, her senses had gone into overdrive, and she was vitally aware of him mere inches away. So much for her hope of keeping detached. It was almost as if fate were conspiring against her.

'Why didn't you?'

'It occurred to me you'd think I was staying behind to seduce Alex, and I didn't want that,' she told him dryly, looking round at him in time to see his lips twitch. 'It was a lose-lose situation, so here I am.'

'So we both end up with the booby prize,' he drawled ironically, steering them carefully around a sharp corner. 'Going back to Alex, I would like to know what you said that brought him hotfoot outside to warn me off.'

'He warned you off?' she asked, startled, and Ransom's lips twitched.

'He seems to think I might make a pass at you. I was tempted to tell him I wouldn't touch you with a bargepole, but then I would have had to explain why.'

Sam winced inwardly at the remark, which notched up another hit on her tattered heart. 'What stopped you?'

'We have an agreement, and, as you haven't broken it yet, my hands were tied.'

It was that simple 'yet' that annoyed her. According to him, it was only a matter of time before she reverted to type and made a play for Alex. Despite all the assurances she had given him. 'You never used to be so doubting,' she complained, only to hear him laugh.

'Knowing you had a profound effect on me. I realised that I was as capable of being duped as the next man. All in all I have to thank a higher force that there was never very much between us. I was able to put it behind me in short order.'

Never was very much between them. Something started

to ache way down inside. That was so untrue. He had been everything to her. God, how she had hated giving him up, but she had had no other option. She would do it again in an instant, given the same circumstances, no matter what pain it gave her.

'Really? You sound awfully bitter for someone who has supposedly "put it all behind you",' Sam was quick to point out.

Ransom cast her a sharp look. 'Seeing you again has dredged it all up. It doesn't sit well to recall I asked you to marry me and you laughed in my face. That all you were interested in was sex.'

Sam gasped in affront. 'It was never just sex!' she denied, the words slipping out before she could stop them.

Ransom's laugh was derogatory. 'It sure as hell wasn't love. You said as much yourself. You can work out the equation yourself. A good thing minus love leaves sex. Which, I have to admit, was pretty explosive stuff. If nothing else, you were a passionate bed mate.'

She stared at his profile, and all the poise in the world couldn't stop hot tears smarting at the backs of her eyes. 'Lord, you really do despise me, don't you?'

He spared her a mocking glance. 'You could hardly expect otherwise. You made a fool of me six years ago, but no woman will get the chance to do it again.'

Her heart contracted. She didn't like the sound of that. 'You can't possibly be tarring all women with the same brush!' she exclaimed in alarm. 'You're going to get married one day, aren't you?' Please God, she prayed silently, don't let me have blighted his life entirely.

'That would depend on finding a woman I could trust. You of all people can understand why I have a jaundiced view of your sex. I've learned to be cautious.'

He wasn't putting her mind at rest at all! 'Don't take caution too far. You'd make a good husband and father.'

'That's rich, coming from you,' he returned scornfully.

Sam couldn't help but resent that. 'OK, I might not have wanted…those things with you,' she snapped, gagging a little on the lie, 'but it never meant I doubted your ability to be a good husband and a good father!'

Ransom's response was to laugh. 'If I didn't know better, I'd think you cared. Don't worry about me. I'll get married when the time is right.'

Ransom turned the Land Rover in through the entrance to a marina, returning the waves of several couples as they drove past. The place was buzzing with people, and it took a while to find a parking space. There he turned off the engine and twisted to face her.

'Tell me something, Sam. Was marriage to a man more than old enough to be your father all it was cracked up to be?' Ransom enquired sardonically. 'Did you grow to love him for himself as well as his money?'

She shook her head, amazed at his sheer gall. 'That's none of your business,' she declared frostily.

Grey eyes narrowed consideringly. 'As the man you threw over in order to marry Grimaldi, I think I have some right to know.'

She knew what he was asking, but she had no intentions of revealing the private side of her marriage. Turning in her seat, she faced him squarely. 'OK, I'll tell you this much. My marriage was all I expected it to be, and caring for Leno was easy to do.'

'That's an interesting way of putting it. You *cared* about him. I would have expected you to insist that you loved him. Especially as he left you all his money.'

That had her glaring at him. 'You know something, Ransom? I don't care what you expected. I had a good marriage!'

'Good enough to make you want to go through it all again? Given the end reward was high enough, of course.'

Her throat closed over as the scorn of his words hit home. 'You have no right to say that. I only lost my husband a short while ago. I still miss him!' she added, because it was true. No matter how the marriage had come about, Leno had been a good man.

One eyebrow quirked her way. 'Yet if I were to kiss you right now, all thoughts of your late husband would fly out of your head like that!' He clicked his fingers to illustrate his point.

It was a remark designed to shock, and it certainly did that. Her stomach lurched at the mere idea, because, God help her, she knew it would be true.

'That has to be the most arrogant thing you've ever said!'

He smiled silkily. 'Maybe, but it doesn't make it any less true. Does it?' His tone was equally silky smooth.

A lump threatened to choke her, and Sam had to work hard to swallow it down. 'The point is moot. You aren't going to kiss me, so we'll never know.'

No sooner were the words out than their eyes met and locked, and she made a shocking discovery. He was considering it! It was there in those stunning grey depths. He was weighing up the odds, deciding if he wanted to go that far or not. She could scarcely believe it, but it had the muscles in her stomach tightening and her nerves sparking. And, in time with her heart, a reckless voice started to urge him to do it. Do it... Do it...

Something in her eyes must have betrayed her, for his smile slowly took on a mocking curve, and his eyes a knowing glint. Then in the next instant he turned away and thrust open the door.

'OK! Let's get this show on the road!' he declared brightly, jumping down and slamming the door behind him.

Sam sagged in her seat, dazed by the last couple of minutes. What was going on? Ransom had actually considered kissing her, and that went against all he had said. It made no sense. He had been quite clear about what he did not want, so why debate kissing her—even to prove a point?

Suddenly, like a jack-in-the-box, his head reappeared in the window. 'Something wrong?' he enquired with barely hidden irony.

Had she been closer, she might just have slapped him for that; as it was she was too far away. 'Only the company,' she retorted acidly, which drew a grin from him before he vanished again.

Feeling distinctly jangly, Sam had no option but to gather her battered armour about her and venture once more into the battlefield that was her relationship with Ransom. Valiantly she picked up her bag and coat and climbed out of the vehicle.

Ransom was collecting his own things from the back. 'Got everything?' he asked, and, at her nod, shut the door and set the alarm. 'The boat's this way.' He jerked his head to the left, swung his bag over his shoulder and walked off.

Blinking at his retreating back, she muttered something dire under her breath and hastened after him. They must have looked extremely odd, with her swaying like the tail of a dog! Uncannily, it was this less-than-gentlemanly behaviour that gradually started to reawaken her sense of the ridiculous, and after a while her lips began to twitch as she followed in his wake. Once or twice she had to skip to keep up, and then had to suppress a fit of giggles. He didn't look round, just expected her to be there—like a faithful hound trotting at his heels. The picture in her mind was so incongruous, a laugh finally escaped her, and Ransom glanced over his shoulder.

'Something amusing you?' he asked suspiciously, and Sam pressed her lips together to stop them from twisting into a grin.

'Uh-uh,' she denied with a shake of her head, and his eyes narrowed.

'What are you up to?'

She gazed back demurely. 'Up to? What can I possibly get up to out here?'

One large hand settled on her shoulder like a ton of bricks, and her knees very nearly buckled. 'If you're thinking of bunking off, you can think again.'

'The thought never crossed my mind,' she denied angelically.

He laughed. 'Right, and I'm a Dutchman! I think it would be better if you were where I can see you. You can lead the way.' His hand steered her ahead of him and shoved her off.

'I don't know where I'm going!' Sam protested, still feeling the warmth of his touch like a brand on this shoulder too.

'Just keep straight on and stop before you hit water,' Ransom advised mockingly.

'Gee, thanks for the warning.'

'And try not to fall over anything,' he added as she almost tripped over a rope.

'What would I do without you?' she responded with heavy irony, and heard a laugh escape him.

'I aim to please,' he came back swiftly, and, because she could hear the grin in his voice, Sam glanced over her shoulder, eyes dancing.

'And we both know how good you are…' she began to say flirtatiously, only to realise just what she was doing. This was exactly the sort of thing they had said to each other back when things had been right between them. She had slipped into the role without thinking. '…at that.' She finished the sentence in next to a whisper, because she saw the flash of mockery in his eyes.

'That's a very provocative thing for a grieving widow to

say to a man,' he goaded. 'You seem to be having trouble remembering you insisted you aren't going to be making a play for me.'

Knowing she had laid herself open for that, she winced inwardly. 'Nonsense. I simply forgot where I was,' she returned quickly.

'Even though you were looking right at me?' he challenged sardonically, and she ground her teeth.

'Maybe I was looking at you, but I was thinking of Leno,' Sam insisted repressively, and without another word she turned and started walking again.

What a stupid thing to say, she berated herself at each step. For one bright instant it had seemed so natural for them to be together, exchanging loaded repartee as they had used to do. It had felt good, and she had forgotten how things had changed. Now he would be bound to think she was coming on to him, when she wasn't.

'Far be it from me to interrupt your thoughts of your husband,' Ransom went on conversationally. 'If you could walk without the sexy wiggle, there would be considerably less temptation around.'

That brought her to yet another halt. 'I do not have a...wiggle when I walk!' she spluttered, rounding on him in disbelief.

His trade-mark wolfish grin was in full evidence. 'You do from this angle, and it's damn sexy,' he shot back, taking her breath away.

'Damn it, Ransom, you aren't supposed to be looking at my backside!' Sam reproved him. What on earth had got into him today? Maybe she was losing the plot, but surely this...flirtation was precisely what shouldn't be happening between them. If he disliked her, why was he doing it?

'I'm a man, not a monk.'

'OK, so try thinking of me as a nun!' she went on in exasperation, only to hear Ransom burst out laughing. Sam watched him double up in a mixture of irritation and despair. He looked and sounded so carefree, it turned her heart over.

When he had recovered somewhat and taken a deep breath, he regarded her wryly. 'Sorry about that, but I don't think I could get into the habit of thinking of you as a nun!' he said with a shake of his head and another bout of laughter.

Though she fought not to do it, his amusement was infectious and in seconds Sam ended up grinning back at him. 'That's an awful pun, Ransom!' she complained, giggling.

'I'm a barrister, not a comedian,' he pointed out, and she pulled a wry face.

'Just as well, or you'd starve.'

Ransom, having finally sobered, pointed ahead. 'It's not much further. Lead on. I promise to keep my eyes on the path,' he said easily. 'Take the next jetty. My boat's moored about halfway down.'

Obediently she followed his directions. 'Does this boat have a name?' she asked.

'Can't you guess?'

'*Saucy Sue*?' she suggested. 'How about the *Pequod*?'

Ransom touched her shoulder and she jumped, glancing round questioningly. 'Try something a little more apt,' he said, inclining his head towards the boat next to them.

Moored there was a sleek yacht, but it wasn't her beauty that caught Sam's breath, it was the name. *The Inconstant Heart*.

'The name pretty much swung the deal. The previous owner had been taken for a ride, too. She had barely been used, but he wanted to get rid of her. We closed the deal right there and then,' Ransom explained, stepping onto the deck and holding out his hand to help Sam do the same.

If she could have got on board unaided, she would have done so, but, being unaccustomed to small boats, large ones too for that matter, she took Ransom's hand, bracing herself for the charge that rippled through her. This time she managed not to give herself away, but, from the glint in his eye, she doubted he was fooled.

'I would have thought you'd have changed the name by now,' she remarked coolly, moving away from him to give herself breathing space.

He gave her an old-fashioned look. 'I couldn't do that. It's too good a reminder of how careful a man has to be,' he retorted mockingly, leading the way down into the cabin. 'Stow your things in one of the lockers. Make yourself at home. Look around. It will take me a while to get her ready for sea. Come up on deck when you're ready.' With that he took himself off.

Sam let out a shaky breath. The last half hour or so had been a shock to the system. Ransom wasn't behaving at all as she expected, and she simply did not know what to make of it. He shouldn't be so friendly and accommodating, and he most certainly should not be flirting with her. OK, so he got in a good few digs at the same time, but he had her unsettled, not knowing quite what was coming next, or from what direction.

He should have been remote, cold. Polite as good manners demanded, but nothing more. She could have handled that. But this… It was as if he had another agenda and was working his way through it. What was it all about, and why? She didn't like it, not one bit, yet she was here now and could only see it through. Hopefully all would become clear eventually.

It took all of five seconds to put her things away, then, taking him at his word, she spent the next fifteen minutes exploring the galley and forward cabins. It was a beautiful boat, and she would not have minded spending time on it had things been different. Eventually she returned to the main cabin, listening to the sounds of Ransom moving about overhead. Should she go up there or stay out of his way down here?

If she stayed down, no doubt he would think she was skulking. Whilst there were advantages in trying to avoid him, the truth was there was nothing to do down here, or see, and he had invited her on deck. Besides, it simply wasn't in her nature to skulk, which made the decision simple. She might even be able to help, supposing he would accept it. At the very least she could enjoy the view.

Ransom was in the process of casting off the moorings, and jumped back on board as she appeared.

'Thought you'd got lost,' was his only remark on catching sight of her.

'Is there anything I can do?' she offered, watching him walk to the cockpit and start the engine.

'All done, thanks.'

Bracing herself as they started to move away from the jetty, she glanced at the still-furled sails. 'Aren't you going to use the sails?'

'Not until we get out of the harbour. I prefer to get out of all this traffic first.'

Sam glanced round at all the boats coming and going. 'It is rather busy.'

Ransom nodded. 'When we've left them all behind, we'll turn off the engine and haul up the mainsail,' he told her with a grin.

She could feel the excitement in him. His joy at being on the water again was almost palpable. 'You love it, don't you?'

His grin expanded. 'Next best thing to sex,' he agreed wolfishly.

'I'll have to let you know about that later,' she returned dryly.

They chugged slowly out of the harbour, and it wasn't until they were well outside that Ransom opened up the throttle and they moved more quickly. It was a little bumpy, but Sam found she liked the feel of the salt spray on her cheeks and the wind in her hair.

'This is fantastic!' she exclaimed in delight, and glanced round to find Ransom watching her with an odd light in his eyes. It vanished before she could decide what it meant.

'Stomach OK?' he enquired.

'Fine,' she confirmed. Except for the fluttery feeling that look in his eye had given her.

'Means you must be a natural. Want to set some sails?'

Sam nodded, always preferring to be hands-on rather than an observer. 'What do I do?' she asked enthusiastically, and it brought that wicked grin back to his lips.

'You look like a little girl who's been promised a treat,' he teased, and she shrugged, laughing.

'I haven't had this much fun since...' Since they had parted, was the honest answer, but as her heart lurched painfully she knew she couldn't admit as much '...oh, since for ever!'

'Then grab hold of that handle and get ready to turn it when I tell you,' he ordered, cutting the engine and going forward. 'OK—now!' he called out minutes later, and Sam started turning. Slowly the sail began to rise. Ransom came back to help with the final few feet, then he took the wheel and edged the boat round until the wind filled the sail, and suddenly they were under way again, only this time it felt quite different.

'Oh, this is much better,' she declared from beside him. 'I can't explain it, it's just...'

'I know what you mean. There's no other feeling quite like it, and once you've been bitten by the bug you'll never escape it,' Ransom agreed, and when their eyes met there was a brief moment of total empathy.

This close she could see fine lines around his eyes, and deeper ones beside his mouth. She wanted to reach out and smooth them away, and had to look away quickly before she gave in to temptation.

'Does this mean I'm going to have to buy myself a boat?' she asked in order to divert her thoughts onto safer ground.

'Sailing lessons first, then comes the boat. I would never forgive myself if I allowed you to drown,' Ransom corrected lightly.

'Especially as everyone says how good a sailor you are,' she agreed equally lightly. 'Do you get to sail much?'

'Not so much as I would like to, but enough to keep me sane in an increasingly insane world.'

'I heard that you'd taken silk,' she said casually, as if she'd come across the snippet of news in passing. The truth was she had followed his career avidly in the press and professional journals. It had made her feel less cut off from him.

Clearly her remark had surprised him for he glanced at her with brows raised. 'Really? I wouldn't have thought you'd be interested.'

She managed a faint laugh. 'Well, I might not have wanted to marry you, but I was happy for you all the same. I knew how much it meant to your career to take silk. It must have been a proud day.'

Ransom nodded. 'It was. Funnily enough, there was a time when I thought having you there would make it perfect. As it turned out, I was wrong. I didn't need you to be happy. Strange how the mind works,' he added ironically.

Wind caught at her hair, and she was able to hide the way the colour left her cheeks at his words by making a production out of smoothing it back down. 'We all have to move on,' she responded levelly, though the hurt lingered.

'Did you imagine me losing sleep over you, Sam?' he asked next, right out of left field, and her nerves jolted.

'Not at all.' She had prayed he wouldn't. She had wanted it to be over for him quickly.

His laugh was scoffing. 'I don't believe you. There isn't a woman alive who doesn't want to think a man is pining for her. It's part of your psyche.'

'I can't speak for the other women you've known, but for myself you're wrong. I wanted you to forget me,' Sam insisted gruffly, and he studied her mockingly.

'To ease your conscience, darling?' he challenged sardonically.

Irritated by his tone, she tipped her chin up. 'Hardly, darling. I've never had a moment's doubt that I did the right thing!' she shot back.

One eyebrow quirked. 'What about a moment's regret? Did you have any of those? After all, we had a pretty hot sex life going there for a while.'

Her chin dropped, for she had never thought he would ask her such a blunt question.

'Are you seriously asking me if I missed the sex?' she asked incredulously.

In response he grinned rakishly. 'Why not? Like I said, you were always an enthusiastic bed mate.'

Her throat closed over, and it was suddenly an effort to force words out. 'No, I did not miss the sex!' she denied through gritted teeth. She had missed *him*. She had ached for *him*. She had loved him, damn it! Pushed just that fraction too far, her emotions threatened to break free, and she knew she had to get away to get them back under control.

Her intention was clear, but her vision was not. She had no idea what she tripped over, but an instant later she felt herself falling. Where she would have ended up she would never know, for a strong hand caught hold of her, hauling her upright and into the safety of a firm male chest.

Sam clung on, and as her world slowly righted itself she became very aware of the heat coming from Ransom's body. At the same time her senses were bombarded by the unique scent of him, and the thudding of his heart beneath her ear. It was aeons since she had been this close to him, and she was overcome by a powerful longing to press closer.

Almost at once she knew it was highly dangerous, that she should be pushing herself away. Indeed, she attempted to do so, but that involved lifting her head, and when she did so she found herself speared on the end of a hot grey gaze. Ransom's eyes flickered with fire, and, scarcely daring to breathe, she watched as his gaze left her eyes and settled on her mouth. Her lips tingled as if he had touched them, and they parted on a tiny gasp as desire sparked into life.

It was as if that tiny sound triggered a release mechanism, and with a muffled sound he lowered his head and took her mouth. There were no preliminaries. One second there was nothing, and in the next white-hot passion. He kissed her with a depth of hunger and need that melted her bones and had her responding instinctively. There was no thought of denial. One large hand framed the back of her head, holding her there whilst he plundered her mouth with a kind of desperation.

Sam had no other thought than to return his kiss with an equal desperation. She gloried in the passion of it, for it had been a long drought, and she had missed him so much. She had hungered for so long, and finally she was being given sustenance. Right or wrong, good or bad had no place here. There was only the stark emotion.

How long it would have lasted—or where it would have led to—was a question doomed never to be answered, for the boat suddenly gave a lurch as the sail flapped, and Ransom let her go in a hurry, grabbing for the helm and restoring the yacht to the correct course.

Left to her own devices, Sam sank onto the nearest seat and tried to get her breathing under control. Her heart was racing like the wind, and the abrupt end to that wildly passionate kiss had left her feeling bereft. Yet, with distance between them, reason slowly started to return, and she began to realise just what a mistake it had been. She should have stopped it, done something, not just let it happen. They had opened a box that should have remained closed, and now temptation was on the loose. Her eyes were drawn to the strong lines of Ransom's profile, and Sam wondered what he was thinking.

She found out soon enough. Having checked that all was well with the boat, he finally looked her way, and the mockery in his gaze spoke volumes.

'What the hell were you trying to prove?' he demanded to know, taking her breath away in a far less pleasant way than just moments ago.

'Me?' she ejaculated, totally surprised by the charge.

One brow lifted, querying her reaction. 'You virtually threw yourself at me.'

The injustice of that brought her to her feet ready for a fight. 'I tripped, if you recall,' she corrected forcefully. 'And even if I hadn't, you didn't have to kiss me. That was your idea,' she reminded him caustically.

'True,' he acknowledged wryly. 'The impulse to know got the better of me.'

'Know what?' she gasped, nerves twitching.

Grey eyes glittered roguishly. 'If it would be as good as before. I think we've pretty much answered that question, don't you?'

Sam stared at him speechlessly. Oh, yes, they knew the answer. It had been good. Very good. But it made no difference to anything. At last she found her voice to point out the pertinent facts.

'That…kiss…was a mistake. One that won't happen again. After all, we don't love each other. This is just…' She hesitated over the word but Ransom had no such squeamishness.

'Lust. We can still turn each other on, only this time there's nothing so fine or noble as love about it. Except, there never was love on your part,' he added, unnecessarily so far as she was concerned.

Already edgy, she snapped a retort. 'Must you keep harking on about that?'

His lips twitched, not quite breaking into that irritatingly mocking smile she was coming to know so well. 'Just making sure we both know where we stand.'

Sam frowned, not sure where this was going. 'I already know that. I'm *persona non grata*. The woman you wouldn't touch with a bargepole!'

Ransom edged the boat round a fraction as he answered. 'Speaking as a red-blooded male, I'd prefer to use my hands,' he said, and if his intention was to confuse her he succeeded.

'To do what? What are you talking about?'

'To touch you with. A bargepole isn't designed for up-close-and-personal contact,' he came back instantly, causing her nerves to skitter wildly.

She couldn't believe she was hearing right. 'What's that supposed to mean?'

'It means, darling, I might be interested in investigating this unfinished business between us after all,' he enlarged, taking her totally by surprise.

'You're not serious!' she exclaimed, heart hammering away fit to bust, and Ransom cast her a sardonic look over his shoulder.

'Never been more so.'

Sam pressed a hand to her forehead in a futile attempt to stop her thoughts from spinning round. 'But you don't—'

'Love you?' he cut in, and now the mocking smile was in evidence. 'You said it yourself. You don't have to love someone to want them.'

Sam folded her arms, staring at his back with dazed eyes. 'Last night you said you didn't want to carry on from where we left off. I remember it distinctly.'

'And I meant it. If we had a relationship, it wouldn't be the old one. I'm not that man any more, even if you're the same woman,' Ransom declared easily, as if they were discussing nothing more vital than the weather.

Sam couldn't seem to stop her heart thudding in alarm. 'It's all hypothetical. It isn't going to happen.'

When he turned and looked at her, there were shadows in his eyes. 'So how does it make you feel, Sam? Happy or disappointed?'

Her chin rose automatically. 'Happy, of course.'

'Of course,' he echoed with a soft laugh. He glanced at his watch. 'Time's getting on. I'm going to bring her about and head back. Unless you have any objections?'

Sam rubbed her arms as a sudden chill swept over her. 'Back is good,' she agreed, and took a seat at the stern, giving him plenty of room to manoeuvre.

Soon they were flying back the way they had come, and Sam watched him work. It almost seemed as if he were part of the boat, so in tune was he with her. Sam felt unnecessary, and knew this trip had been a mistake in more ways than one. Above all he had staggered her with the implications of what he had just said, and, in all honesty, she didn't know exactly how she did feel, except sad.

Ransom was suggesting they could have a relationship of sorts. One that wouldn't involve love, only passion. Would she want that? Could she accept it? She didn't know. All she was sure of was that her life had suddenly got a great deal more complicated.

CHAPTER SIX

Once back at the marina, it took very little time for Ransom to make the boat secure, and in less time than it took to say it they were in the car and driving back towards the house. They didn't say much to each other on the homeward journey, and it was only because Sam was keeping her attention focussed out of the window, not on the man in the driver's seat, that she suddenly caught sight of Alex.

They had paused at a road junction near a beautiful old country pub, and she was busily admiring the building when she became aware that sitting outside it at one of the tables was Alex.

'Oh, look! There's...' Sam started to say, with the intention of calling to him, when out of the corner of her eye she saw a young woman come out of the pub door. That in itself wasn't unusual. What stopped Sam in her tracks was the fact the woman went to join Alex. Within seconds their two heads were close together as they engaged in what was obviously a very private conversation.

'...Alex,' she finally completed the sentence, eyebrows raised in mild surmise.

She had managed to draw Ransom's attention away from the traffic flow. He glanced round, and when he followed her pointing finger his eyes widened. 'Well, I'll be damned!' he exclaimed, just as an irate toot from behind alerted him to the fact that the road was clear. With an apologetic acknowledgement, Ransom quickly set the car in motion.

Sam frowned as she turned to look at him. 'Do you know

who she is?' she asked, and he spared her a quick look laden with irony.

'I haven't the foggiest idea, but they were certainly cosy. I imagine she was an old friend.'

A cheeky smile flickered across her face. 'A very old friend,' she agreed, and saw his lips twitch.

'A very old, *close* friend,' Ransom amended on cue. 'I'm curious. Just how much has Alex told you about his past involvements?'

Sam sighed, irritated by the implication of his question. 'Nothing at all. We don't have that kind of relationship. As I've tried to tell you many times. It's probably safe to say he has secrets like the rest of us,' she pointed out reasonably.

Ransom glanced at her with a provocative grin. 'Can't argue with that, can we?'

Sam's nerves leapt at his insinuation that there were still a lot of secrets waiting to be uncovered. 'Speak for yourself!'

He laughed mockingly. 'Liar! I tell you what. I'll tell you mine if you tell me yours. What do you say?'

She sent him a scornful look. 'I say you'll wait until hell freezes over!'

All he did was laugh some more. 'Sam, Sam, you are so predictable! Anyway, getting back to Alex. Karl did tell me that his brother had been heavily involved in the past.'

'Do you think that's her?' she asked, her curiosity piqued by what she had seen.

Ransom shrugged. 'Who knows? That little tableau may have been entirely innocent.'

Sam frowned as she considered that, then rejected it. 'Except she was almost sitting on his lap!' she pointed out dryly.

'I wondered if you'd noticed that. Perhaps he'll bring her

back to the house. Seems to me the next few hours could turn out to be very interesting.'

When they reached the house, Sam hurried up to her room to shower and wash her hair. Feeling a great deal more comfortable, she slipped into a pair of cut-off trousers and a fashionable strappy top. Back downstairs, the Hunts' housekeeper, Mrs MacFee, had laid out a late lunch for them on the patio. Ransom, she discovered when he joined her, had showered also and donned cream chinos and a pale blue shirt with the sleeves rolled up.

To Sam he looked heartbreakingly attractive, and it was hard to concentrate on the food on her plate. Her eyes kept wanting to watch him, and the one time she caught him raising his glass of chilled white wine to his lips her thoughts immediately brought up the kiss they had shared. It had been as good as before, just as he had said. So good she wanted more. Yet more was out of the question. Wasn't it?

Immediately she slammed the door shut on the thought. But the damage was done. Oh, Lord, if she could think that way, she was in trouble!

She groaned silently and prayed for a diversion. Almost immediately she heard voices inside the house. Sam cast a questioning look at Ransom, who shrugged and sat back in his chair, an odd smile hovering about his lips. Seconds later two figures emerged from the house. Sam wasn't surprised to see Alex with the woman from the pub, but her brows rose fractionally when she saw they were holding hands. So that was the way the wind blew.

Alex looked totally at ease as they approached the table. 'Hi, you two. What a morning! I bumped into an old friend, Emma St John, and we've been talking over old times. Emma was at a loose end, so I invited her back for lunch. Ransom Shaw is an old friend, and Sam Grimaldi is visiting with my mother.' He made the necessary introductions.

'Hello there, Sam, Ransom,' Emma declared, with a friendly smile, holding out a hand across the table, which they both shook in turn.

Sam smiled back. 'I hope you're both hungry. Mrs MacFee has excelled herself. We'll need help if we're to make a dent in all this food. Help yourself.' She waved her hand towards the dishes of salad and cold meats spread across the table.

Ransom rose and with a charming smile helped Emma to a seat, and Sam instantly felt her smile grow tight. It was jealousy, pure and simple. Which was ridiculous, because she had no claim on Ransom whatsoever.

Ransom returned to his own seat, whilst Alex took a spot between Sam and Emma. Mrs MacFee arrived to set two extra places, bringing a fresh bottle of wine and some glasses with her.

'Thanks, Mrs Mac. You've done us proud, as usual,' Alex complimented her, and with a broad smile she vanished back into the house.

'So, how long have you two known each other?' Ransom asked the question Sam was eager to know the answer to as well.

'Oh, it must be about four years, would you agree, Alex?' the other woman replied, helping herself from the dish he held out to her. As she did so she held the dish steady with her free hand, and her fingers brushed his.

Anyone not watching as closely as Sam would have missed it. They would also have missed Alex's and Emma's eyes meeting for a fleeting instant. Sam observed the byplay with gentle amusement. So far as she was concerned, volumes had just been spoken. These two felt deeply about each other. She was happy for them, and hoped it would work out.

'About that,' Alex confirmed, piling food onto his plate. 'We met when I advised her on her finances when they were in a bit of a mess. We've bumped into each other from time to time, but I was totally gobsmacked to find her in this neck of the woods.'

'I'm only here for a few days with friends,' Emma explained. 'I never expected to run into Alex. This is so amazing!'

'You can say that again!' Alex exclaimed, then went bright red as he realised how much feeling he had put into the words. 'Anyway, how did you two get on? I can see you didn't drown,' he teased Sam. 'Did you have a good time?'

'It was great fun. I nearly fell once, but Ransom saved me.' Which was about all she was prepared to reveal of the happenings on the boat.

'I told you Ransom was the man for the job,' he reminded her jauntily, and Sam smiled faintly.

'So you did,' she agreed, turning her attention to the food on her plate.

The next hour passed in a pleasant blur of chatter and laughter, and it felt to Sam like a moment out of time. She couldn't recall the last time she had laughed so freely from real enjoyment. Of course, it couldn't last, and before long Emma said she had to leave and Alex went with her to drive her to where she was staying.

The minute they disappeared from view, Ransom let out a soft whistle. 'Call me crazy, but I'd say that pair are well and truly smitten,' he declared with satisfaction.

Sam glanced his way, grinning. 'I don't think they just bumped into each other, do you?'

'Not a chance,' he returned with a laugh, and she nodded.

'I'd say Emma did a lot of groundwork in order to just bump into him today. Whatever happened in the past, she isn't going to let him go this time!' Sam joined in the friendly laughter.

'Looks like you just lucked out,' Ransom told her, and she frowned in confusion.

'Excuse me?'

He jerked his head in the direction the other couple had gone. 'You might have had him in your sights, but Alex was already spoken for.'

Sam couldn't be bothered to respond to the jibe. 'Believe it or not, I'm happy for him. If he wants Emma, and it's pretty clear what she wants, then good luck to them. They deserve to be happy.'

One brow quirked her way. 'What about you?'

'What about me?' she tossed right back at him.

Ransom crossed one leg over the other and made himself comfortable. 'Is it time for plan B?'

Sam grimaced and closed her eyes for a second before looking his way. 'I know I'm going to regret asking, but what exactly would plan B be?'

Mockery danced in his eyes as he answered. 'Looking for the next available man with more money than sense.'

She shook her head helplessly. 'You're like a dog with a bone! Don't you ever give up?'

'Giving up is not part of my genetic make-up,' he told her, stretching lazily.

Her eyes followed the movement, and she was struck by a pang of longing to be able to touch him as freely as she had once been able to do. She glanced away, knowing it was one of those things that was gone for good. 'It's probably what makes you a good QC,' she told him.

Ransom's hand settling over hers where it lay on her lap gave her nerves a severe jolt. She shot him a startled glance, because the gesture was so unexpected. He smiled that lazy smile that had always been able to set her pulse racing. It did the same now, which was probably why she didn't immediately jerk her hand free.

'What do you say we take a walk down through the

wood? It's a nice afternoon for it,' he suggested, surprising her yet again.

Common sense told her he was unlikely to be seeking her company for its own sake. No doubt he had something he wanted to say to her in private, and didn't want to be surprised by the family returning. Whatever his motives, she felt too restless to sit here any longer. A walk would help to restore her equilibrium.

'Thank you, I'd like that,' she agreed, getting up.

Sam followed where Ransom led, not bothered which way they went. They strolled down through the garden and out through a concealed gate to a deeply rutted lane, which meandered into the wood just ahead of them. It was pleasant and quiet, with nothing but the birds' songs for company.

'You know there's no way on God's green earth that I would have let you make a play for Alex, don't you?' Ransom said conversationally after some time had elapsed.

Sam wasn't surprised by the question, she had been half expecting something like this. 'I do. You were very clear on that point, as I recall,' she responded dryly.

Ransom picked up a fallen branch and shifted it out of their path. 'That was then. I have different reasons now for putting a stop to it,' he explained casually, dusting off his hands before slipping them into the pockets of his trousers.

Now he had surprised her. 'Is that so?' she queried, wondering what she had done to earn his disapprobation. 'I suppose you're going to tell me eventually,' she added sardonically.

'In fact, I would stop any relationship you tried to make,' he went on calmly, causing Sam to come to an abrupt halt. That was taking things too far, as she was about to point out.

'You couldn't. And even supposing that you could, why would you?' she wanted to know.

'Because you and I have unfinished business. Our outing this morning proved that to both of us,' Ransom returned levelly, and Sam's nerves skittered violently at the unnecessary reminder.

'Some business should be left unfinished,' Sam insisted, though she knew she would be haunted by the memories of today for a long, long time. 'We shouldn't even be having this conversation,' she added edgily. 'I'm crazy to be talking about it at all.'

He looked at her, and she was transfixed by his smouldering gaze. 'No, you're not,' he denied that. 'The best way to describe you is pure temptation on legs,' he added huskily, sending a shiver down her spine.

Her breath caught in her throat at the unexpected turn of the conversation. Quicker than winking, the air surrounding them became positively charged, and fraught with possibilities. Caught off guard, she held up her hands as if to ward him off, although he hadn't moved.

'Just hold on a second. What are you doing?'

Grey eyes danced. 'What do you think I'm doing?' he countered provocatively.

She knew well enough, but it shouldn't be happening. She was off limits. 'Just…stop. OK?'

'I would, but I have a problem,' he said softly, taking a step towards her. She backed up.

'What problem?' she asked, and silently cursed the husky quality to her voice.

Their gazes became enmeshed, and that exhilarating connection was made instantly. Tiny shivers ran along her flesh as she saw the heat in his eyes.

'A memory problem.'

'M-memory problem?' She knew she sounded like a parrot, but couldn't help it.

'Um-hmm. You see, I have a perfect memory, and I can recall how satisfying it was to make love to you. You were

uninhibited. Wildly passionate. It would be so easy to get
lost in you.' Ransom took another step, which she matched
to keep the distance between them.

It was a remark that set her senses reeling and her temperature rising, for she hadn't forgotten how it had been
either. 'Maybe, but it isn't going to happen again,' she
pointed out, taking another backward step.

He laughed with wry humour. 'Fine words, but this thing
between us never worked that way. If I touched you, you'd
melt. Just as you did this morning.'

Oh, she knew what he meant only too well. Being this
close to him was far from relaxing, and that kiss too close
in memory for comfort. She had melted then, and probably
would again. Where he was concerned, she was a hopeless
case. Which didn't mean she wasn't going to put up a fight.
He was playing a game with her, and she needed to keep
a clear head to figure out where it was leading.

'We agreed that was a mistake.'

'It could be a mistake we're doomed to repeat,' he insisted, tipping his head to glance around her. 'You might
want to stop there,' he cautioned.

Sam looked round and realised she was at the top of a
small depression. She swung back to face him with a firm
denial. 'We won't be repeating anything!'

'You're wrong.'

Her stomach lurched, for she hadn't allowed herself to
think along those lines yet. 'How can you be so sure of
that?' she asked breathlessly, though she knew the answer
well enough.

'The fact that we still want each other changes things,'
he said, not pulling his punches.

Sam shook her head in disbelief at what was happening.
'This can't be happening! When I woke up Friday morning,
everything seemed so simple. Somebody up there really
doesn't like me!'

'Or has other plans for you,' Ransom suggested helpfully.

The possibility of that made her temperature rise. 'I'm not interested in other plans. I'm certainly not interested in finishing this unfinished business between us!' she fired back, and turned to put some distance between them, completely forgetting the dip behind her.

Sam took one step, slipped and landed on her bottom, slid some distance like that, then rolled the rest of the way. She finally ended up face down in a pile of old leaf litter that had been settled there by the wind. With a heartfelt groan of frustration she stayed where she was, head cradled against her arms, wondering if the day could possibly get any worse.

She heard the slithery sound of Ransom coming down to join her, but didn't look up.

'Are you OK?' he asked, and there was no mistaking the laughter in his voice.

'I'm perfectly fine, thank you for asking,' she replied caustically, still not looking at him.

'What were you trying to do?' he asked, hunkering down.

At that she raised her head and spat out a piece of leaf. 'A double somersault in the piked position. What do you think I was doing, you…you…? Aargh!'

'I'd certainly give you an A for effort, though you could do with a little work on the start,' he responded, trying not to laugh whilst grinning from ear to ear in unholy amusement.

There was a part of her that responded to his boyish charm, but because she really didn't want to laugh right now she gritted her teeth. 'Don't laugh at me, Ransom,' she threatened, twisting into a sitting position, brushing aimlessly at the debris clinging to her clothes.

'Or what?' he came right back with the dare.

Pushed, she tightened her fingers on handfuls of leaves. 'Or this!' she exclaimed and chucked the large handfuls at his grinning head.

She caught him by surprise, but only for a second. As she started to laugh he wiped the muck from his face. A dangerous glitter entered his eyes. 'Right!' he roared, taking her on, and within seconds the air was thick with leaves as they proceeded to bombard each other.

Ransom had a longer reach and better aim, and Sam soon realised she was getting the worst of it. No fool, she made a bid for escape, but as she started to scramble up the slope on all fours Ransom caught hold of her ankle and tugged her back down.

'Oh, no, you don't!' he growled, and to make sure she didn't try it again he held her down with his own weight, one leg thrown over hers to keep her where she was. 'OK, darling, now what are you going to do?' he challenged, bracing himself on one elbow so he could look down at her and counter any move she made.

Not that Sam was considering making any moves. The laughter slowly faded away as she became very aware of his body lying over hers. It was very intimate, reminding her of other times. Her mouth went dry, and instinctively she moistened her lips. A tiny action, which nonetheless drew his attention and within seconds he, too, had stopped laughing.

Sam could hear her racing heart thundering in her ears, and she knew she must not look at him, for if she did she would be lost. But where to look? Every way seemed to lead towards another source of temptation—his head, his thigh, his hands. In the end, she focussed her gaze on the top button of his shirt.

'I think you should let me up,' she suggested scratchily,

not daring to push at him, for she knew that that would be a big mistake. Touching him would only make her want more.

'You can think at a time like this?' Ransom challenged, equally huskily, and of course her reaction was to look at him.

The instant she did, getting out of the situation scot-free vanished. Their eyes met, and the ability to think clearly was the first casualty. There were banked fires in his eyes that drew her, warmed her, tantalised her. Once she had been able to stir those embers into a raging fire that she had been quite happy to burn up in.

Without conscious volition, her hands rose to rest against his chest. 'Oh, Ransom,' she sighed, achingly soft, desperately needy.

He made a purely male sound deep in his throat. 'Oh-h-h, yes,' he murmured, and, without wasting another second, brought his mouth down on hers.

It was beautiful. Nowhere near as desperate as that earlier kiss, and yet more powerful. It awoke a hunger that was fuelled by every nip of teeth and stroke of tongues. Sam's fingers curled into the silky fabric of his shirt and held on tight, whilst Ransom's free hand sought the edge of her tee shirt and slipped beneath, fingers splaying out over the velvety skin of her back. She sighed with pleasure and arched against him, feeling his body stirring against hers. Her own responded swiftly. Her breasts ached to be touched, whilst the throbbing deep inside her cried out to be eased.

At which point a dog barked and a child called out, laughing, and they both froze. An instant later Ransom rolled off her and sat up, whilst Sam lay staring up through the leafy canopy, trying to get control of her breathing. She had barely managed to do that when a small black-and-white dog hurtled into view, shortly followed by a boy of about ten. He stopped, startled to find them there, but the dog bounded over to Ransom, his tail wagging so hard he stirred the leaves.

'Hey, what's your name?' Ransom asked the inquisitive canine, scratching him behind the ears to evident delight.

'Come here, Buster. Here boy,' the boy commanded, and the dog reluctantly bounded away. 'Sorry,' he apologised. 'We didn't know anyone was here. Hope he didn't scare you.'

'No problem. I like dogs,' Ransom responded with a smile and the boy nodded.

Then he glanced from Ransom to Sam, who had sat up now and was picking off bits of dead leaf. 'Er...are you OK? I can get my dad if you need help,' he offered.

'We're fine. We got tired walking and sat down for a while,' Ransom explained easily, and fortunately the boy accepted that, though he grinned widely.

'OK,' he replied cheerily. 'Gotta go. Come on, Buster!' he encouraged the dog and ran off with the dog yapping at his heels.

Leaving Sam and Ransom alone again.

'Well, that was as effective as a cold shower,' Ransom remarked humorously as he clambered to his feet and started to brush himself off.

Sam rose too, though less elegantly. She tried to comb her fingers through her hair, but it was a mess of tangles and leaves. 'I'm glad you think it's funny!' she exclaimed. 'If that dog hadn't barked he would have walked right in on us!' She had never been so mortified in all her life.

'And found us kissing. Big deal.' Ransom swiftly put the situation into perspective. Walking over to her, he attempted to pick some pieces out of her hair, but Sam swung away.

'He shouldn't have found us doing anything,' she insisted, whereupon Ransom caught her by the shoulders and turned her round.

'Stop fussing over nothing. And stay still!' he added as she made to move away. Dextrously he managed to rid her hair of the debris in no time at all. Then he started to brush at her back and bottom, but that was going too far.

'Cut it out! You've touched me enough for one day!'

Ransom folded his arms. 'I didn't do anything you didn't want me to do,' he pointed out reasonably, which Sam couldn't argue with.

'Well, thanks, that makes me feel a great deal better,' she retorted sourly. 'Look, let's get one thing clear. There is to be no touching, no…funny business of any sort in future. Stay away from me. Whatever game you're playing, leave me out of it.'

There was no laughter in his eyes this time as he looked at her. 'I don't play games. And whatever this is, you're a part of it, like it or not.'

Her heart skipped several beats at that pronouncement. 'You can't want this!' He might want her, but he had no deep feelings for her, and she didn't know if she could bear the coldness of that despite the heat of their passion for each other.

He dragged a hand through his hair. 'I certainly didn't plan for it, but I'm a realist. I'll play with the hand I'm dealt.'

The lack of real emotion in that brought a lump to her throat. 'What if the stakes are too high?'

'I don't think we have a choice.'

Sam shook her head in swift denial. 'Of course we do. We could just walk away.' It would be the sanest thing to do. There would be less pain—for her at least.

Ransom inclined his head in acknowledgement. 'We could, but then we would never know, would we?'

Her heart lurched. 'What do you mean?'

'We'd never know if the game was worth winning.'

A shiver ran down her spine despite the warmth of the

day. 'What is there to win?' Not his love. She had lost that a long time ago, and there was no retrieving it. She wasn't a coward. She would risk everything if she thought there was a chance. Yet she knew without doubt that there was none.

'We wouldn't know that till we got to the end,' Ransom answered with a shrug. 'You have to decide if the journey would be enough. I'm going to do my best to convince you that it is. Besides, what have you got to lose?'

More than he would ever imagine. Yet, for all her denials, she was tempted. Would the journey be enough? She wanted him, true, but would having him cause her less pain in the end?

'What do you hope to gain?' she asked him, because that was the crucial question, and he smiled with self-mockery.

'To get you out of my system once and for all. Right now you're like a fever in my blood that I can't shake off. You're the only one who can cure me,' he told her in a husky voice that trickled over her skin like butterfly wings.

'I could make you worse instead of better,' Sam pointed out, and he shrugged again.

'It's a risk I'm willing to take. You want me, Sam, and you don't even have to pretend to love me to get me this time,' he urged, flashing his rakish smile at her.

His words hit the target he hadn't even aimed at, and Sam let out a ragged breath of laughter. 'You mean I can have my fun without paying for it?' she managed to ask in a silky tone, whilst the wound to her heart bled silently.

'Absolutely,' he agreed, and she drew in a deep breath. Determined not to let him see her pain, she smiled faintly. 'Then I would be a fool not to consider it, wouldn't I?'

Something flickered at the back of his eyes and was gone in an instant. 'I knew you'd see it my way in the end.'

Sam made no answer, for there was no reply to that. At

least she had a clear idea of what their relationship would
be—should she agree to it. No love, no deeper feelings,
just red-hot passion for as long as it lasted.

Ransom walked on and Sam followed, her thoughts deep
and not especially pleasant. She had the distinct feeling that
her life was about to take yet another unexpected turn, and,
for the life of her, she couldn't honestly say whether she
would be happy or sad.

Sunday turned out to be another scorcher. After breakfast
Alex proposed that Sam and Ransom should join himself
and Emma at the beach. They could get in some swimming
before returning to London in the afternoon. For once
Ransom left the choice up to her. Probably because he
knew that she wouldn't be able to find a good reason not
to go. Which turned out to be the case.

She agreed, and went upstairs to gather her things together with the memory of Ransom's twinkling grey eyes
laughing at her predicament. It wasn't that she didn't want
to go, it was the seemingly natural pairing of herself and
Ransom that had her nerves doing the high jump. There
was something preordained about it that left her vaguely
shaken. As if the future were already set, despite the fact
that she didn't know what she was going to do about
Ransom and their reawakened mutual attraction.

The beach wasn't too crowded, and they managed to find
a fairly quiet spot. As soon as the towels were laid out,
Alex and Emma stripped down to their swimming things
and ran for the water. Ransom simply removed his tee shirt,
leaving his tanned body and limbs covered by his disrep-
utable shorts.

As he dropped down to the towel beside Sam and
stretched out his long, muscular legs she couldn't keep her
eyes from wandering over him, and her throat closed over.
He was the epitome of male perfection, and, as ever, her

fingers tingled with the urge to explore him, to discover if he felt the same as she remembered. Her mouth dried up and all at once it felt as if her blood were pulsing slowly through her veins.

Her gaze wandered upwards across his powerful chest, and eventually reached his face. Whereupon she discovered, with a jolt, that he was watching her through brooding eyes.

'Enjoying the view?' he enquired dryly, and yet there was a heat in his gaze that defied the irony.

Colour washed into her cheeks, but she remained outwardly cool. 'You always were good to look at,' she told him levelly, calmly removing her shorts and top to reveal a one-piece bathing suit.

His lips took on a wolfish grin that raised the hairs all over her body. 'You don't have to stop at looking, you know. In fact I'd welcome the touch of your velvety hands right about now,' he added, taking her breath away.

'Stop it!' she ordered, stifling a groan that was the measure of her sudden need to touch him as he wanted.

Rolling sideways, he used one arm to prop himself up. 'I'm not actually doing anything.'

Sam shot him a narrow look. 'You're flirting with me,' she accused, and he laughed.

'Is that what I'm doing? Funny, I thought I was attempting to seduce you. Anyway, it isn't a crime to want you, darling.'

Unable to hold the power of his eyes, Sam looked away, picking up her bag and rummaging in it for sunblock. 'Just because everyone seems to be pairing us off, doesn't mean it's a fact!'

'Not yet, at least,' Ransom agreed, taking his gaze from her to study Alex and Emma playing in the waves. 'They make a good-looking couple.'

Sam, who had been about to make a pithy reply to his

remark, glanced up from smoothing the cream onto her legs to follow his gaze. 'Yes, they do,' she said softly, and more than a little wistfully.

Emma had joined them for dinner last night and had been a hit with the Hunts from the word go, which was what Sam had expected.

'They're young and in love. Everything is perfect for them,' she went on, hoping it would stay that way. It was a result of her own pain that she wanted everyone else to be happy.

Ransom turned his head to look at her. 'Do you envy them?'

Her heart squeezed. Of course she did. But for fate that could have been herself and Ransom. 'I envy them their happiness. I can remember what it felt like.' She glanced at him, smiling ruefully. 'To be young and in love is special.'

'Who were you in love with?' he asked curiously, and her stomach lurched as she realised she had said too much.

'It doesn't matter now,' she said repressively. Abandoning the sunblock, she lay down on her stomach and closed her eyes. Silently she prayed that he would let the matter drop.

He didn't. 'I take it the man had no prospects. That must have hurt. Of course, you could have been poor and happy, but that obviously wasn't what you wanted.'

The sarcasm in his voice stung as never before, and she came up on her elbow, eyes blazing. 'You know nothing about what I wanted, Ransom, so leave the past alone! It's over, done, and nothing can change it! So just…drop it, will you?' she exclaimed angrily, before lying down with her head turned away from him.

Damn, damn, damn, she thought silently. She had just overreacted big-time. Lord, but her nerves were in a mess.

The only good thing was that he would never for a second think she was talking about him.

'I'm sorry,' he said after a long moment had passed, and it surprised her so much she just had to look at him.

'Are you apologising?' she asked incredulously.

His smile was wry. 'It's not unheard of,' he responded and she laughed.

'Around here it is.'

Ransom shrugged, easing his shoulders as if there was tension there. 'I tend, from my own experience, to forget that you weren't born a gold-digger. That came later. What happened to the love of your life?'

Sam wondered what he would say if she told him the love of her life was sitting right beside her. She let out a long, sighing breath. 'Life happened to him, Ransom. Just life. The thing that happens when you're making other plans. Now, if you don't mind, I'm going to lie down and forget all about the past.'

She did just that, doing her best to ignore the man beside her. She succeeded for all of five minutes, then received a sharp awakening when she felt his hand on her back.

'What...?' she began, trying to get up, but his hand firmly pushed her down again. 'What are you doing?' she spluttered as his hand began to run lazy circles over her skin.

'You'll burn, so I'm putting some cream on your back. Lie still or you'll get sand on it,' Ransom warned her, not pausing in his task.

She could feel the glide of the cream then, but all she was stunningly aware of was the brush of his hand on her flesh. It was so long since he had touched her, even as innocently as this, and her eyes closed, forehead dropping down to rest on her hands. His touch was like magic, sending chills of pleasure along all her ultra-receptive nerve ends. The pleasure was so keen that she had to bite her lip to hold back a moan. Did he know what he was doing to her? She thought not—until his fingers grazed down the side of her ribs, tips just catching the curve of her breast. She gasped, thinking she had imagined that it was done on purpose, but when it happened again, this time more lingeringly, she knew he knew what he was about.

Yet she couldn't make herself stop him. She wanted to feel this—needed it. When his hand finally came to rest at the small of her back, she felt bereft.

'Don't stop,' she heard herself say in a croaky whisper.

'It's either stop or make love to you in the full view of everyone on the beach,' Ransom told her in a voice made raspy with desire.

Sam turned over, staring up at him as he looked down at her. She lifted her hand until it rested over his heart and felt the thunder of its rapid beating. 'Oh, God!' she groaned helplessly.

The heat in his eyes was hotter than the sun. 'It isn't going to go away, Sam.'

'I know,' she admitted, knowing she was lost.

Ransom brought his forehead down to hers and closed his eyes. 'I want to kiss you so damned much, but I know if I do, I won't want to stop.'

Sam said nothing, for what could she say? It was the wrong time and place. She was just trying to summon up the strength to push him away when the job was done for her.

'Well, well, well! What's going on here?' Alex exclaimed from right beside them, and Sam jumped as if she had been stung.

Ransom sat up slowly, running a less than steady hand through his hair. Sam sat up too, the heat in her cheeks having nothing to do with the sun. They both looked at Alex, who was standing with his arms akimbo, laughing heartily.

'How long has this been going on?' Alex chortled until Emma thumped him on the arm. 'Ow! What was that for?'

'Men!' Emma exclaimed, exchanging a wry look with Sam, who shook her head and scrambled to her feet.

'Never mind. I need to cool off anyway,' she added with a cheeky grin, and quickly jogged down to the water, wading in until she could dive into the next wave.

The swim worked wonders, cooling down her overheated blood. Finally, when she began to tire, she flipped onto her back and floated lazily. Alex's interruption had been timely, but ultimately it changed nothing. Ransom was right: this physical attraction wasn't going to go away. They wanted each other still, and it was a powerful pull. Of course, on her side there was also love, which wasn't true for him. She must never forget that. Still the big question remained—what was she going to do?

She really had no idea, and right then it was too hot to think about. Instead she swam back to shore and joined the others. She was careful not to sit too close to Ransom, a fact he noted with a twist of his lips. She was vitally aware of him though, even when she was chatting to Emma. It wasn't uncomfortable; it was simply an electric tingle in the air. She was attuned to him as to no other person in the world. It was her fate.

They swam and sunbathed for the next few hours, but eventually the tide came in, so they packed up their things and returned to the house. Ellen and David Hunt were sitting out on the patio under the shade of an umbrella, drinking tall glasses of something that looked deliciously cold.

'What's that you're drinking?' Alex wanted to know.

'Fresh lemonade,' his mother responded. 'You'll find a couple of jugs made up in the fridge.'

'I'll get it,' Sam offered immediately. Not giving anyone a chance to argue, she headed for the door to the kitchen. She would make up a tray and take it out to the others, then she would come back and wash off all the salt and sand she had collected along the way. In the kitchen Sam went to the large refrigerator and took out a jug of lemonade. Setting the jug on the counter, she rustled up a tray and set about hunting for some tall glasses. Once they were found, a quick recce through the cupboards produced crisps and biscuits.

Picking up the tray, she was just about to walk out with it when, to her horror, a large spider appeared over the edge and made a dash straight for her. Sam's reaction was immediate. With a sound somewhere between a screech and a scream, she let go of the tray and jumped back at the same time. Seconds later the tray fell to the floor with a deafening crash. The spider who had caused it all scuttled off in the opposite direction and vanished.

Very aware that she was soaked with lemonade, and probably generously covered with slivers of glass, Sam didn't move. She heard voices call out, and could picture everyone jumping to their feet. Seconds later Ransom rushed into the kitchen, closely followed by Alex.

'What happened?' Ransom charged, stopping on the edge of the disaster area.

'I dropped the tray,' Sam explained, feeling a complete and utter idiot.

'I can see that,' he returned dryly. 'The question is why.'

Sam licked her lips, knowing she had to own up. 'Well, you see, there was a spider on the tray and it startled me. So I dropped it. I'm sorry. I'll pay for the breakage.' This last was directed towards Alex.

Ransom grinned and Alex started to laugh.

'You mean Ransom ran to your rescue like the proverbial white knight, for a spider?'

'You don't know how scared she is of spiders,' Ransom responded, and Alex's eyes widened.

'No, I don't. How do you?'

Sam looked at Ransom, wondering how he would get out of that. Simply, as it turned out. 'It came up in conversation.'

If Alex didn't quite believe that, he wisely kept his own counsel. 'Look, if you can manage here, I'll go and tell the folks everything's OK.' Taking their agreement for granted, he loped out again.

'Good footwork,' Sam complimented Ransom, and his quirky grin appeared.

'It helps to get you out of situations you've got yourself in,' he added sardonically, surveying the mess around her. 'Stay where you are, Sam. I'm going to lift you onto a chair, and then get that glass off your legs.'

He was as good as his word, lifting her off her feet with ease and depositing her on the nearest chair. There were one or two tiny pieces of glass stuck in her, but he managed to pull them out and clean up the rest with the minimum of fuss.

'There you go,' he declared, standing up. 'Where do they keep the mop?'

'I think the broom cupboard is over there,' Sam pointed to a door in the corner. 'There could be one in there.'

Ransom caught a broom that toppled out when he opened the door, then set it back inside and took out the mop and bucket. The way he filled it and set about clearing up the mess told her he was no stranger to menial tasks. In no time at all he had the floor cleaned up, returned the mop and bucket to their cupboard and produced two glasses of lemonade from the remaining jug in the refrigerator. Sitting down opposite her, he pushed a glass her way.

'So, how has your day been so far?' he asked tongue-in-cheek, and Sam laughed.

'Not without its moments of high drama. I never knew lemonade could spread so far, or be so sticky,' she returned with a delicate shudder.

'You don't look overly upset by the way things have turned out,' he remarked idly, yet watching her response closely.

'You mean with Alex and Emma? I did tell you I wasn't interested in him that way. You ought to listen more,' Sam was quick to point out.

'My wise old gran used to say you learn more with your ears open and your mouth shut.' Ransom nodded wisely.

Sam frowned, not sure whether to believe him. 'Does she exist, this wise old gran of yours?'

'Still going strong at ninety,' he confirmed with a low-wattage smile that still managed to tug at her heartstrings.

'Then she's doing something right. Perhaps you ought to follow her advice,' she suggested and he laughed wryly.

However, before he could say more Alex returned with Emma in tow. 'Sorry to interrupt, but we're going to grab a quick shower and change of clothes then go out for lunch somewhere. Would you care to join us?'

Sam blinked in surprise. 'I thought we were planning on getting an early start home,' she said awkwardly, and hated to see Alex's smile falter.

'That's right, we were. Damn,' he muttered under his breath.

'I'm heading back to town myself shortly, so I can drop you off if you like,' Ransom suggested, and Alex's smile reappeared.

'There you are, you see, no problem,' he declared brightly, then caught the look in her eye. 'That is, if it's OK with you, Sam?' he added hastily.

What could she say? It simply wasn't in her to deny him this time with Emma. 'It's OK, I'll accept Ransom's offer.'

'Thanks. I owe you one,' he said with a charming smile, then he and Emma disappeared into the house.

Sam turned to Ransom. 'Are you sure it's OK? I can go

by train if it's too much bother,' she offered, needing to give him an out.

A faint smile curved the corners of his mouth. 'Like I said, we're both heading in the same direction. Besides, we have a lot to talk about.'

She wasn't sure she liked the look in his eyes as he said that. 'We do?'

'I've no intention of ignoring what lies between us,' he reminded her softly, and a shock wave went through her system, causing havoc with her senses. She didn't believe she could ignore it either, but neither was she going to rush into anything.

'I have no intention of jumping blindly into a relationship with you, Ransom,' she informed him coolly.

He smiled slowly. 'That's OK. I'm a patient man. I can wait.'

Even feeling about him as she did, it still made her blood boil that he would assume she would be there whenever he wanted. 'You might wait for ever!'

'I doubt it, but if you want a battle, I'm game. The close-quarters fighting might be interesting!' he declared with a laugh, and got to his feet. 'Why don't you go up and pack whilst I go and tell Mr and Mrs H about the change of plans?' he suggested.

Sam watched him walk outside, her mind seething. If he thought she would simply fall into his hands like a ripe plum, he had another think coming. She might want Ransom as much as she ever had, but she was no pushover. As he was going to find out. She wasn't going to jump at a snap of his fingers.

Ransom was only interested in an affair, and although to say yes would give her more time with the man she loved above all others, it wasn't what she really wanted. Just because she knew she couldn't have that, did it mean she should settle for what he was offering?

It was a situation she was going to have to think about very carefully.

CHAPTER SEVEN

THE telephone rang on the reception desk beside her, and Sam almost leapt a foot off the ground. She was getting positively jumpy, and all because of a six-foot hunk of man. Ransom had driven her home as he had promised he would, and had left her at her door with a casual: 'I'll be in touch.' That had been over two weeks ago, and she hadn't heard a word from him since. To make matters worse, instead of feeling relieved that the threatened battle of wits had not materialised, she was getting more and more rattled.

Every time the telephone rang at home, or the doorbell sounded, she expected it to be him. When it always turned out to be someone else, her spirits actually sank. A feeling she promptly counteracted by getting annoyed that he hadn't rung and allowed her to refuse whatever plans he had.

Knowing him, she couldn't rid herself of the sneaking suspicion he knew what she was thinking and was deliberately staying away. Whatever the reason, the outcome was the same. She was fast becoming a sorry mess, constantly lurching from one emotion to the next.

Consequently when the phone rang this time she snatched up the receiver and answered far more curtly than she usually would. 'Royal Hotel.'

'Tsk, tsk, tsk... Who got out of the wrong side of the bed this morning?' that unforgettable voice enquired mockingly, and her heart lurched wildly before galloping off madly.

Her immediate thought was a profound relief that he had finally called. Not because the waiting was over, but because she had secretly started to wonder if he had changed his mind. A reaction that illustrated just how mixed up she was. However, now that he was on the end of the line, instinct insisted she reveal nothing of her vacillating state of mind.

'How did you get this number?' she asked shortly.

'It was in the phone book. Ellen kindly told me where you worked. I admit to being surprised. Why are you working at all?'

'I can't believe you rang to play twenty questions, Ransom,' she replied coolly, deliberately avoiding answering. For added privacy she moved along the reception desk, not wishing to be overheard by staff or guests.

Like her, he chose not to answer, but asked another question. 'Have you missed me?'

Does night follow day? she groaned silently.

'I've scarcely given you a thought, as it happens,' she lied. Of course she had missed him. She had been missing him for six years, and, looking at it now, she realized her reaction these last few days had been because she had desperately wanted him to call. She had needed to know that it wasn't all over. That she could refuse and still have the opportunity to change her mind. If that wasn't mixed up, it sure came close!

Ransom laughed softly. 'Yes, me too,' he confirmed, sending her heart thumping.

That old magic started to wreath itself around her, but Sam was still determined not to respond to his charm too easily. 'I'm sorry, was there something you wanted? Because if not, we are rather busy...' She let that hang on the air, pleased she sounded cool and efficient.

'Liar!' came the one-word answer.

Taken aback, she gasped. 'I beg your pardon?'

'As well you might,' Ransom continued, tutting. 'There's

only one person at the desk, and he's being ably seen to by one of your colleagues.'

Sam jerked the receiver away from her ear as if she had been bitten and scoured the lobby frantically. If Ransom knew there was only one man at the desk, then he had to be... She caught sight of him sitting totally relaxed in a chair over by the window, looking as if he had been there some time. He waved his mobile phone at her and turned it off as he stood up. Sam ground her teeth in frustration. It was so like him to play such a trick on her, and what she felt like doing was chucking the receiver at him. What she did do was set the phone down and stand tapping her nails in an irritated tattoo on the desk whilst he approached.

Annoyed she might be, but that didn't stop her senses responding to the sheer vitality of him. She was aware that female heads turned as he walked by, but his attention was set firmly on her. He was telling everyone in the vicinity that there was only one person he was interested in right now, and that was a turn-on without equal. Her blood began to flow thick and hot through her veins, and her mouth became dry as a desert.

Not that she was about to reveal the effect he had on her. 'What are you doing here, Ransom?' she demanded in a frosty voice when he finally reached her.

'Now, now,' he reproved provokingly. 'Is that any way to talk to a customer?'

'You're not a customer, you're a pest,' she corrected smartly. 'What do you want?'

His smile was like a blast of pure sensual energy and turned her legs to jelly. 'You.'

Sam was temporarily set back on her heels by that. It took quite an effort to concentrate her mind, for her senses wanted it to follow wanton lines of thought. 'Really? Maybe if you hadn't taken two weeks to get in touch with me, I might be impressed,' she told him coolly, raising a challenging eyebrow at him.

Ransom's reaction was to widen his smile. 'Getting worried, darling? The answer is simple. I gave you two weeks' grace. I had a feeling you would think it indecent haste for me to come calling too soon. Your annoyance tells me I was wrong, but I'm prepared to make up for lost time now.'

His answer satisfied a lot of unspoken questions. He was right; she would have been uncomfortable with a swift approach from him. However, that didn't mean she was about to hand herself over to him as a reward for his thoughtfulness.

'I'm afraid that's out of the question, so if there's nothing else…'

'Actually, there is,' Ransom countered smoothly. 'I came to take you to lunch. When I rang earlier, one of your colleagues was kind enough to tell me you were taking a one o'clock lunch today.'

She stared at him helplessly. 'They had no right to do that,' she pointed out, wondering who it could have been. Everyone knew better than to give out any information, however innocent.

Ransom merely grinned unrepentantly. 'Don't blame them. I can be very persuasive. It's part of my job to get the reluctant to speak.'

He was right. She doubted if anyone could resist him when he was determined. 'I'll have to warn them to be on their guard against you in future.'

One eyebrow lifted. 'So, there is to be a future. I'm glad to hear it.'

Sam narrowed her eyes at him warningly. 'I didn't mean it like that and you know it.'

'Hmm, sounds as if you need feeding. You always did get grumpy when you were hungry,' he went on as if she hadn't spoken. 'Let's go. I happen to know of a great place just around the corner.'

It was maddening that he took her acceptance for granted. 'I'm not going anywhere with you. I'd rather starve!'

He shook his head at that. 'Now you're just being silly,' he reproved as if she were no more than five years old.

Which understandably made her blood boil. 'Now just a minute...' she started to say, and only then became aware that all was quiet around her. Glancing round, she discovered that she was the centre of attention behind the desk, and that she was being observed with various degrees of amusement. Colour stormed into her cheeks, and she heartily wished the ground would open up and swallow her whole. Of course it didn't and, to save herself from more embarrassment, she did the only thing she could.

'I'll just get my bag,' she muttered, and made good her escape.

In the staff room she took a deep breath and pressed her hands to her cheeks. Her whole body was atremble, and that had nothing to do with making a fool of herself. It was all due to Ransom. No matter what she said, she *was* eager to see him. Which kind of made a mockery of all her fine words about fighting him. Her resistance was little more than a sham. If he really tried he could break it down with the touch of a finger, she was that needy.

However, she had her pride and would go through the motions, for he had a big enough head as it was. Keeping that in mind, she told herself to calm down, ran a brush through her hair and checked her make-up before hanging her bag from her shoulder.

When she went back to the lobby, Ransom was waiting by the door. There were a few moments when he was unaware of her approach, and she was able to see his profile. He looked...pensive. Brooding almost, and she was just wondering if it was to do with a case when he must have sensed her approach and turned. He smiled, and as she was caught in the sunshine radiance of it that odd moment was forgotten.

Ransom took her to an exclusive and popular restaurant, where he would have had to book a table.

'You were so sure I would agree?' she remarked sardonically, which made him grin.

'I was sure I was going to eat here, whether you joined me or not,' he countered smoothly. 'However, I am glad you chose to come.'

Somehow he always managed to say the right thing, Sam thought wryly. 'It wasn't as if I was given much choice. The staff were hanging on every word, and you used that,' she accused him, glancing at the menu she had been given.

'I told you all was fair in love and war. I intend to use every advantage I have to get you where you want to be,' he told her in such a huskily sensual voice her stomach turned over and all the fine hairs on her skin stood up.

She knew she shouldn't ask, but did so anyway. 'And where is that, exactly?'

'In my bed.'

Her mouth suddenly went dry, and she had to lick her lips to get a word out. 'My God, Ransom, you assume a lot on the basis of a couple of kisses,' she declared gruffly, trying to sound mocking, but merely sounding breathless.

'Oh, I base it on more than that, darling. I base it on my intimate knowledge of you. All the little signs that tell me what you really mean, despite what you say,' he responded seductively, setting her pulse racing once more. 'We want each other. We will share a bed again. Only the time and place remains to be settled.'

Sam looked away, pretending to read the menu, though the words were little more than a blur. How could she deny it? Of course she wanted him. She loved him. He was everything she wanted, would ever want. Yet she wanted all of him, whilst he only wanted a physical relationship. However satisfying that might be, ultimately it would only hurt her more. When there was nothing to hold them together, when all passion was spent, he would leave her. How could she do that to herself?

On the other hand, how could she deny herself this unforeseen gift of time with him?

'Sam?'

She jumped, coming back to earth from miles away, startled eyes flying to meet his intense grey ones. 'Sorry, did you say something?'

'Are you ready to order?' he repeated, and only then did she realise the waiter had returned and was hovering beside them. Never caring to eat much during the day, she ordered a Caesar salad and coffee. Ransom chose the same, and the waiter vanished.

'So, are you going to tell me why you're working at the hotel?' he asked, changing the subject, much to her relief.

Sam shook her head with a little sigh. 'If you must know, I needed to be busy. Not just busy, useful. I help people every day, and I like that. You probably thought I was living a life of idleness and luxury,' she finished caustically.

'Only until I learned about the hospice project,' Ransom enlightened her. 'Ellen was only too happy to tell me about it. She sings your praises from the rooftops.'

Sam was warmed by what he told her, but at the same time it made her uncomfortable. 'I'm just one of many trying to help those less fortunate. I know Leno would be pleased with what I'm doing. He was always generous to good causes. I wanted to continue that.'

Ransom sat back in his chair and eyed her consideringly. 'You work. You give money away. Seems to me you've had something of a sea change. What happened?'

'Maybe I saw the error of my ways,' she replied with a shrug.

'Hmm, maybe,' he agreed thoughtfully. 'The world moves in mysterious ways. Who would have thought you would have said goodbye to your husband such a short time ago, and then run into me again? Not a bad deal, when all is said and done.'

If she really had him, which she wouldn't have. 'You can hardly compare the two situations, Ransom. We're not talking permanency here, are we?' she responded as casually as she could, though the subject was a painful one. No amount of wishing would give her what she truly wanted.

'I certainly won't be asking you to marry me this time, if that's what you mean,' he confirmed, leaning forward, arms resting on the table. 'Our futures lie elsewhere, but we both know we're still in each other's systems. We need closure, Sam, darling, and there's only one way to achieve it. We're suffering from a fever in the blood, and we have to let it run its course so it can burn itself out.'

Her heart tightened. From his point of view it was totally logical, but for her… She would never have enough of him. Two lifetimes wouldn't even scratch the surface.

'What if it backfires? What if I was to fall in love with you instead?' she couldn't help but ask, and it hurt when he laughed.

'We both know there's no danger of that. Love is something you wouldn't understand.'

Sam drew in a pained breath, knowing she had got what she'd asked for by asking the question. 'I must seem awfully shallow to you,' she said unevenly, to which Ransom shrugged dismissively.

'You can't help being what you are.'

'Then why have anything to do with me at all?'

'Because the fire is still raging, and cold showers don't work,' he admitted wryly.

'You aren't afraid of getting burned?' Sam asked huskily, knowing if she went into this, she would never have to worry about betraying her feelings, for Ransom would never think them more than window-dressing.

He grinned roguishly. 'I can cope with getting a little singed around the edges!'

'So long as you can walk away free of the baggage from the past?' she drawled mockingly.

'What reason have you got to say no?' he challenged with the utmost confidence, and she could have told him she had the best one of all. Because she loved him.

Yet in her heart of hearts she knew that, despite her protestations, there really was only one place she wanted to be. That place was wherever he was, and under whatever circumstances. When push came to shove, she wasn't too proud to take any crumb she could, for it would have to sustain her for a very long time.

'It's all so easy to you, isn't it?' she countered huskily, and he shrugged.

'That's because it is. You want me, Sam. You can try to deny it, but we both know it would just be words.'

She sighed, angling her head in wry acknowledgement. 'You're right, I can't deny it, but…it just seems so…cold-blooded somehow.'

'Sitting here talking about it, maybe. However, memory tells me it will be anything but cold-blooded. At the right time, everything will feel perfectly right. Or would you rather I threw caution to the wind and made mad, passionate love to you right here on the table?' he countered with a quirkily angled eyebrow.

Sam couldn't help but laugh softly. 'You know I never found exhibitionism a turn-on.'

Something smoky and dangerous flickered in his eyes. 'I remember,' he said softly. 'Yet when we were private, you held nothing back. So we'll simply wait until we're alone and see what happens.'

If it was anything like last time, the world would catch fire. 'What if nothing happens? What if I changed my mind? Would you take no for an answer?' she asked, holding her breath. He had always respected her decisions in the past, but had that changed?

She need not have doubted. 'Of course I would. I've never forced a woman in my life, and, even given our situation, I'm not about to start with you,' he said firmly, then smiled wickedly. 'Besides, I know that you will be saying yes eventually.'

Sam was torn between amusement and irritation. 'Your confidence could be misplaced.'

'Care to bet on it?' he challenged with a rakish glint in his eye that warned her not to do anything so rash.

'I don't believe I will,' she refused as calmly as her skittering pulse would allow.

Ransom inclined his head, smiling wryly. 'A wise move.'

The arrival of their lunch brought a welcome interruption. Ransom didn't refer to the subject again, and she guessed it was because he believed it was all settled. Being honest, she knew it was. She wasn't going to walk away, for it would take more strength than she had. This time she would stay until *he* told her to go.

Ransom walked her back to the hotel an hour later.

'I'll pick you up at seven this evening. I have tickets for that new play everyone's raving about. We can get something to eat afterwards,' he informed her as he flagged down a passing taxi.

'Maybe I don't want to see a play tonight!' Sam argued in exasperation, in answer to which Ransom simply pulled her into his arms and dropped a brief but lethally passionate kiss on her lips.

'Don't cut off your nose to spite your face, Sam, darling!' he said as he let her go again. Climbing into the waiting taxi, he lowered the window as it moved off. 'Seven. Don't be late!'

Sam stared after him, feeling a little dazed. By the kiss as much as anything else. She touched her lips, which still tingled. He certainly had a persuasive argument, she thought wryly. She was arguing solely for effect, and it was time to stop. Which meant she *would* be going to the theatre tonight, she told herself, then grinned. Just as well she had been eager to see it all along.

The play was every bit as good as the reviews had said it was, and Sam walked out of the theatre brimming with good spirits. When Ransom took her hand as they walked along the pavement, heading for a nearby restaurant, she was surprised but made no objection. It felt good. Right. As if everything were back as it ought to be. Of course, she knew it never could be, but there was no harm in dreaming tonight.

This time they went to a small Italian restaurant. Ransom ordered drinks whilst they waited for their food, and Sam sat back in her chair sipping at a perfectly chilled white wine, feeling happier than she had for a very long time. Sighing, she raised the glass to her lips again, and caught sight of Ransom watching her. She raised her eyebrows questioningly.

'Can I take it you enjoyed the play after all?' he taunted softly, and she laughed.

'You can. It was brilliant. Thanks for inviting me,' she said honestly.

His eyes danced roguishly. 'You're welcome, but I did have an ulterior motive when I asked you out tonight,' he told her, and she couldn't stop her nerves from leaping as her gaze flew to his.

'You did?' she ventured cautiously.

'A friend has given me the use of a cottage in the Cotswolds. I was hoping to persuade you to join me there for the weekend,' Ransom explained, not taking his eyes from hers, and Sam's nerves gave another wild jolt.

'You're asking me to go away with you?'

His smile was at once audacious and alluring. 'We could do with the privacy, and I can pretty much guarantee that we'd both benefit from the time alone,' he went on persuasively.

That was certainly one way of putting it, but she wasn't sure she was quite ready to take the next step. Which was funny, because the first time round she had had no doubts. It wasn't as if this were going to be something new. They had already had an intense physical relationship, so she knew what to expect. Maybe it was simply that this time she knew from the word go it wasn't going to last.

Sam shook her head dazedly. 'This is rather unexpected,' she declared jerkily, and Ransom reached across the table and took her hand.

'Not so very unexpected, surely? We're both adults. We know what we want. Why should we wait? We're both free agents now.'

The gentle rubbing of his thumb backwards and forwards on her skin was very distracting, not to mention arousing. 'I don't like to be rushed,' she argued huskily, taking a ragged breath in an attempt to control her breathing.

'I remember. You always did prefer to go slow. OK, I'll take as long as you like, darling, but I don't want to wait any longer,' he countered with a husky sensuality that melted her bones and her resistance at the same time.

'I'd forgotten just how persuasive you can be,' Sam groaned helplessly, removing her hand and ending the tactile torment.

'Does that mean you'll come?' he charged swiftly and she forced herself to be sensible.

'It means I'll think about it. You can wait a few days, can't you?' she challenged, unable to stop herself wondering what the rush was for. Yes, she wanted him quite badly, but anticipation was a powerful aphrodisiac in itself.

Ransom sat back in his chair with a rueful smile. 'Of course. As I recall, you were definitely worth waiting for.'

Sam's smile was faintly mocking as she picked up the menu and opened it. 'Good. I was beginning to wonder if I was going to have to pay for my supper,' she said dryly, and gave her attention to the culinary delights listed before her.

'Pay how?' he asked quickly, and there was an unexpected sharpness to his tone.

She lowered the menu enough to look over it. 'I have no idea. What is the going rate for a trip to the theatre and supper?' she asked him sweetly, and clearly saw anger flare in his eyes.

'Now that was uncalled for, darling.'

Sam sighed. 'You're right, and I apologise, but I had to know.'

'You should have known better,' he pointed out with a long look, and she met his gaze and held it.

'How could I? You aren't the same man I knew six years ago. You're harder. Less trusting.'

He laughed softly. 'Well, as the saying goes, you only have yourself to blame for that, Sam, darling.'

Her heart squeezed at the unnecessary reminder, and she felt compelled to say something. 'It was such a long time ago. Aren't you ever going to forgive me?'

Ransom's expression turned solemn. 'I forgave you a long time ago, when I realised you can't change human nature. I was the one at fault for expecting too much. You cannot give what isn't there. Your loss, not mine.'

It was hardly a flattering thing to say, but she supposed she should be thankful for small mercies. At least she was forgiven. However, she couldn't help being hurt by the fact that he never appeared to have doubted what he had been told. OK, so she had played her part well, but if he had known her as well as he thought he did surely a doubt could have crept in? Not that she would have wanted him to have doubts at the time. Which was why she was in this catch 22 situation. She couldn't have it both ways.

'As you say, my loss. Can we order now?' she added, changing the subject, and, taking the hint, Ransom raised his hand to signal the waiter.

The remainder of the evening passed off smoothly enough, and Ransom drove her home before midnight. Parking the car outside her flat, he switched off the engine and turned to face her.

'If I asked for a cup of coffee, would you invite me in?' he asked her tauntingly, and Sam shook her head emphatically.

'Not for coffee or anything else.'

'Then I guess I'll just have to make do with a kiss,' he decided, and before she could say yes or no his hand snaked out, slipping around her neck and pulling her towards him until his lips found hers.

After which the question was academic. She didn't protest because she was too busy kissing him back. Ransom's kisses had always been as addictive as any drug, and she had been hooked on him long ago. She uttered a low moan as his tongue sought hers, deepening the passion until her heart was thundering in her ears, and her blood was pounding through her veins. There was no question of one kiss being enough, and it led to another and yet another. Finally it was Ransom who called a halt by pushing her back into her seat and setting his hands on the steering wheel where they would not reach for her again.

'You'd better go in before I lose all control,' he told her in a voice made thick by passion.

Sam moistened bruised lips and was instantly aware of the taste of him. Her throat closed over, and, unable to speak, she simply reached for the door latch and climbed out of the car, shutting it carefully behind her so as not to make too much noise. As she did so the electric window wound down.

'I'll call you tomorrow,' Ransom said huskily.

She nodded. 'Good night,' she murmured equally huskily and hurried up to the entrance door before she could do something silly like invite him up after all. Once inside her flat, she didn't immediately turn on the lights, but instead walked over to the window and looked out. Ransom was still parked outside, and she wondered what he was thinking.

Her own thoughts were chaotic after those passionate minutes in the car, yet as she stood there watching the stationary vehicle her pulse rate settled and thinking became easier. Ransom had surprised her with the invitation to go away with him for the weekend. She hadn't expected it because it smacked of intimacy. Not fooling herself, she knew that all he wanted from her now was sex. He would see spending the weekend together as the perfect way to finally extinguish those lingering embers of attraction that had taken him unawares. He wanted it over, whilst she...

Well, she wanted him, for ever, but that wasn't going to happen. All the love was on her side. They did not want the same thing. Any decision she made had to be done with that in mind. She would have to compromise. If she couldn't have what she wanted, what would she settle for? The answer to that was easy. What she would settle for was this bonus time with him.

The telephone rang, and Sam jumped, turning to look at it in consternation. Expecting it to stop ringing, when it didn't she hurried across the room and snatched up the receiver.

'Why didn't you turn the lights on?' she was asked by the caller.

'Ransom?'

'Who else would be calling you at this time of night?' he acknowledged wryly, and she wondered if she might not have fallen asleep and was dreaming. A quick pinch proved she was awake.

'Do you know what time it is?' she demanded to know.

'It's gone midnight, which means technically it's tomorrow. I told you I'd ring you tomorrow,' he declared conversationally, and she could imagine him leaning back in the comfortable seat of his car, talking to her on his mobile phone.

'You're crazy!' she spluttered.

'Not yet, but I certainly will be if you don't soon put me out of my misery. Have you made up your mind yet?'

Sam caught her breath in disbelief. 'When I said I wanted time to think, I meant more than a few hours!'

'Take pity on me, darling. I'm due in court in the morning and I need my sleep, but I won't be able to sleep for wondering what your answer will be,' he cajoled her, and she closed her eyes helplessly.

'You're not playing fair, Ransom!' she complained without any real sting in her complaint.

'I told you I wouldn't. Are you going to tell me?'

Sam sank onto the sofa and curled her feet up under her. 'I ought to make you wait.'

'But you aren't going to.'

'You don't deserve it.'

He laughed softly. 'I'm still waiting.'

She hesitated, even though she had just been thinking about what she was going to do. If she agreed she would be taking a step onto the path that would lead to their parting, but that was going to happen sooner or later anyway.

This was not a long-term relationship, so she had to make the most of what she was being offered.

Taking a deep breath, she crossed her fingers, trusting she wasn't about to make the worst mistake of her life. 'OK, Ransom, I'll go away with you,' she told him, and heard nothing but silence from the other end of the line.

'Thank you,' he said finally, with the strangest inflection in his voice. 'Good night, Sam,' he added, then ended the call.

Sam slowly returned the receiver to its rest. She had just burnt her bridges and there was no going back. She only hoped she wouldn't come to regret it.

CHAPTER EIGHT

THERE were times in the intervening few days when Sam wondered if she was really being sensible. The trouble was, loving someone wasn't always about being sensible. When doubts crept in, as they inevitably did, she had to remind herself that she was lucky to get this second chance.

It will be fine, she kept telling herself, like a mantra, but when Friday arrived her nerves were distinctly jittery. It was hard to concentrate on work, and when she got home she wished she hadn't packed in the morning, for that would have given her something to do except wear a path in the carpet and chew her nails.

However, when the doorbell rang a few hours later, her nerves simply vanished. She felt cool and in control as she went to answer the door. One look at Ransom, casually dressed in pristine jeans and denim shirt, one arm stretched out to the wall taking his weight, and the world righted itself. When he smiled, she smiled back and just like that the doubts evaporated.

'Your carriage awaits,' he declared lightly, and Sam handed him her small case. 'Is this all?'

She laughed. 'It's only two days, but I added a good book in case time begins to drag.'

His brows curved upwards. 'Is that a challenge, darling?'

Sam made sure she had her bag and a light fleece jacket with her before she closed her door. 'Only if you see it that way.'

Ransom took her arm as they started down the stairs. 'Trust me, you won't even read one word of it,' he promised, making her laugh again.

'We'll see.'

He made no response to that, although she did catch sight of a gleam in his eye as he helped her into the car. It sent a thrill down her spine. It *was* going to be fine. She had been saying so all along.

The cottage was in darkness when they finally arrived later that night. They had had to contend with several long hold-ups due to holiday traffic, which had added hours to the journey. It was as well Ransom knew the way for the stone building was set at the end of a narrow lane. When Sam climbed out of the car, she was pleasantly surprised to hear a stream rippling over stones nearby.

Now that they were here, her confidence of before began to dip. She started to feel decidedly awkward, because they had come here for one reason only, and she wasn't sure how they should go about it. It was one thing to decide to spend the weekend together, but they couldn't simply walk indoors, jump into bed and spend the whole of the time there! Well, actually, they could, but it was suddenly a little too cold-blooded for her.

Her stomach lurched as she watched Ransom walk up the short path to the door. He unlocked it with a key he produced from his pocket and reached inside to switch on a light. Immediately a golden glow of warmth spread out towards her and what had been cold stone walls turned into a welcoming cottage. Ransom disappeared inside, and she took a deep breath and followed him, finding herself in a large cheery room with an enormous stone fireplace at one end, and comfortable-looking furniture. Her spirits rose a notch.

Ransom reappeared through a doorway on the left. 'The kitchen's through here. Simon hires someone from the vil-lage to keep the cottage clean and stock the fridge whenever they plan a visit. We won't starve, that's for sure. I've put the kettle on. Are you hungry?'

His mundane chatter was reassuring. and she realised she was hungry. Nerves had stunted her hunger earlier, but now she was ravenous. 'I could make us some sandwiches,' she offered, grateful for something to do. 'Would you prefer tea or coffee?'

'Tea, please. Coffee would only keep me awake. Whilst you do that, I'll get the bags from the car and take them up to the bedroom. By the way, just in case you need it, the stairs to the bedroom and bathroom are through that door.' He pointed to a wooden door with a metal latch.

'What, no late-night trips to the bottom of the garden?' Sam joked and he grinned.

'You'd only end up in the stream if you tried it. This place has all mod cons, so you won't have to keep a torch handy,' he told her in some amusement and went back outside.

Sam wandered through into the kitchen. It was another large room with a flagstone floor. The freezer she discovered in a walk-in larder, whose shelves were stacked with tins. The fridge was in the kitchen, together with an Aga, which she didn't have a clue how to use. Fortunately she didn't have to for sandwiches, and she busied herself collecting what she would need, discovering where the cutlery and china were kept by trial and error. Humming softly to herself, she began to put the sandwiches together.

She only glanced up when she heard footsteps on the stairs and then the creak of floorboards as Ransom presumably went into the bedroom. She paused with the bread knife poised to cut into the loaf as her stomach flip-flopped. One bedroom, which she would be sharing with him later. The thought sent her nerves skittering, and she had no idea why, when this was not a new situation for her. They had shared a bed countless times, and she was just being silly.

With a shake of her head, she bent to her task, making a round of sandwiches each and a hot mug of tea. When she carried it through to the other room on a tray, Ransom had come down again and was lounging on the settee. The front door was shut and the curtains pulled, closing them into a tiny world where only they existed. He rose and took the tray from her, setting it down on the coffee-table, then urged her to join him on the settee. When she hesitated fractionally, he sent her an old-fashioned look.

'I'm too tired to pounce on you, Sam. You're safe for the moment,' he jibed, and, feeling foolish, she sat down beside him.

'I didn't expect you to jump on me,' she hastened to point out as she handed him a plate of sandwiches. He took it and started to tuck in.

'Something's got you spooked. Have I changed into a monster in the last six years?'

Sam nibbled away at her own sandwich. 'Of course not! You couldn't be a monster if you tried!' she denied that strongly, making him smile.

'I'm glad to hear it, though I hardly expected such an impassioned defence.'

She shrugged to show her indifference, although she knew she would never be indifferent to him. 'The truth is the truth.'

'Ah, yes, the truth,' he mused thoughtfully. 'They say the truth can set you free, yet in my profession the truth often sends people to prison. Have you noticed that in our everyday lives we have to go on faith that people are being truthful, yet we know there are occasions when a white lie is better than the truth? It's an individual thing. Do you, for instance, always tell the truth?'

Sam tensed at the unexpected and, in her particular case, uncomfortable question. Instinctively she wanted to ignore it, but knew she wouldn't be allowed to get away with saying nothing. 'I do my best to,' she said carefully.

'But you'd be prepared to lie?' Ransom interrogated further.

'If the circumstances required it,' Sam admitted, wishing he would drop the subject, but not surprised that he didn't.

'Really?' he murmured consideringly. 'I'd be interested to know what those circumstances would be.'

Sam looked at him sharply, whilst inside her nerves were jangling with unease. 'Why do I feel like I'm being given the third degree?' she charged, and caused his eyebrows to lift.

'There's no need to get defensive. It was an idle question,' Ransom countered mildly, though she doubted if he ever really asked idle questions. For a man in his line of work, asking pertinent questions would become habit.

'If it's an idle question, you don't really need an answer!' she returned smartly, then had an idea. 'I tell you what. Why don't you tell me under what circumstances you think I would lie?'

'OK.' He nodded, taking up the challenge. He eyed her consideringly for some time before speaking. 'I believe that above all you would lie to protect someone from whatever you believed would hurt them.'

Sam derived scant comfort from the accuracy of his response, and it was all she could do not to react. His insight was uncanny. It was almost as if he knew what had happened six years ago. Yet he couldn't know. She had made certain of that. All it was was a lucky guess, yet it rattled her enough to make her incautious in her reply.

'I'll agree I wouldn't allow someone I cared about to be hurt by something if I could prevent it, but that's hardly unique.' She waved it away with a slightly off-key laugh. 'I mean, there must be hundreds of people out there who would do the same thing!'

'Thousands, probably,' Ransom agreed easily, setting down his empty plate and reaching for his mug of tea. 'As a matter of interest, how many people that you care about have you lied for?' he went on, watching her over the rim of his mug as he drank.

Sam went still, suddenly aware that she had wandered into a minefield and had no idea where it was safe to tread. 'I never said I had lied. We were having a hypothetical conversation,' she reminded him, rather too huskily for comfort.

'True,' Ransom said with a faint smile curving his lips. Sam couldn't be sure, but for a second she could have sworn it carried a hint of...had it been satisfaction?

Having been on the receiving end of the conversation, she decided to turn the tables. 'So what about you? Do you always tell the truth?'

Amusement danced in his eyes. 'Like you, I try to.'

'But you'd lie if you had to?'

'Sometimes there's no other way,' Ransom agreed. 'As you would appear to have found out for yourself.'

Sam finished her sandwich and reached for her own mug of tea with a dismissive shrug of her shoulders. 'It's all in the past, and I have no intention of resurrecting it for your entertainment.'

Laughing, Ransom set his empty mug aside and angled himself on the settee so that he could watch her easily. 'Would I be entertained?'

She smiled, holding his gaze. 'We'll never know, will we?'

His eyes danced. 'Damn, but you're stubborn!' he exclaimed, yet didn't sound in the least annoyed by it.

'I believe you'd call me a hostile witness,' she returned slyly, but Ransom shook his head.

'Right now, the words that spring to mind are pure temptation,' he told her with a look that scorched.

Instantly the atmosphere in the room changed. The air became charged and fraught with untold possibilities. Sam's mouth dried up at exactly the same moment that her heart began to quicken its pace. She couldn't think of a thing to say, which gave Ransom a great deal of amusement.

'Don't look so surprised, Sam, darling. I may be tired, but all my senses are working.'

'I'm not surprised,' she denied at once, turning away from him and stacking the plates and mugs back on the tray.

'But you are uncomfortable,' he went on, setting her nerves on edge because she *was* uncomfortable. She didn't know how to go about having an affair with him. She knew it sounded crazy, but it was true. Last time they had been in love, and it had all been so natural. Now... Well, now she just didn't feel at ease.

Which was why she thought it would be a good idea to do the washing-up. So she rose to her feet, picked up the tray and made a swift exit without giving him so much as a sideways glance. Of course, the instant she was out of the room she felt like an utter fool. Setting the tray on the table, she sighed heavily. Ransom would think she was a complete idiot, and he would be right. The trouble was she was feeling all the things she hadn't felt the first time round! That would have been the time to feel nervous and uncertain, not now.

With a groan of disgust, she carried the crocks to the sink, turned on the hot tap and added a squirt of washing-up liquid. So intent was she on what she was doing, she didn't hear Ransom enter the room, and the first intimation she had that he was there was when his arms slid around her waist and gently hauled her back against him. She tensed, but with her hands in the frothy water there was nothing she could do to alter the situation.

'Relax,' he ordered softly against her ear, his breath stirring her hair, sending tingles down her spine. His lips brushed against her neck, and Sam's eyes closed as a tiny gasp of pleasure left her lips. Slowly her head fell back, and his roving lips found her pulse. His tongue flickered over the frantic beat and like magic the tension in her muscles began to dissolve.

'What are you doing?' she asked breathlessly as his mouth traced the line of her jaw.

'Setting your mind at rest,' Ransom answered huskily. 'Feels good, doesn't it?' he went on, one hand finding the hem of her top and gliding beneath it, caressing her skin to scintillating effect.

'Mmm,' she sighed, raising one bubble-covered hand and sliding her fingers into his hair, loving the silken feel of it.

'So there's nothing for you to feel uncomfortable about, is there?' he murmured, whilst his roving hand continued its exploration, cupping her breast in its lacy covering and teasing the jutting nipple with his thumb.

Sam could no longer recall a single moment of unease, for the practised caress of his hands and lips swept her mind clean of all unnecessary baggage. His touch was the same, and so was her response. It was natural and right, and no other considerations mattered. She would worry about the future tomorrow—whenever tomorrow came.

It was as if a weight were lifted from her at last, and she turned in his embrace, wrapping her arms around his neck, tipping her head to look up into smoky grey eyes.

'I'm sorry for behaving like an idiot. I don't know what came over me,' she said, nipping at his chin with her teeth, then salving the imaginary wound with a caress of her tongue.

Ransom's hands framed her head and he kissed her with a passion that blew her mind. All she could do was respond to it, riding the surge of need it evoked. When he finally lifted his head, they were both breathless.

'Ghosts of the past haunt us both, Sam. Hopefully we can put them to rest for ever this weekend,' he declared huskily. 'We have to move on.'

Her heart ached. To move on to a new beginning, there had to be an ending, and she knew now that that was what this weekend was all about for him. She didn't mind, for this time together was more than she had ever hoped for, even if it could never be enough.

She swallowed a lump of emotion in order to answer him. 'I'm all for moving on.'

'Good,' he acknowledged with a smile, releasing her. 'Now, why don't I finish the washing up, while you go up and get ready for bed?' he suggested.

Her stomach lurched in a mixture of anticipation and nerves. 'OK,' she agreed, and left the kitchen to mount the stairs with a thumping heart. As she collected her red silk nightdress and headed for the bathroom, which housed a positively enormous claw-foot bath, she felt almost giddy.

Two days was hardly any time at all, but she was going to cram a lifetime into what she had. No wailing or gnashing of teeth. She was going to enjoy herself, for she had nothing to lose and only memories to gain.

There was a shower over the bath, and she used that as it was so late. Then she dried herself, slipped into the nightdress and padded back to the bedroom. Ransom had not come up yet. She could hear him downstairs locking up, and knew it would only be minutes before he joined her. Ransom had left the main bedroom light on, but she switched it off in favour of just the one bedside lamp. Satisfied with the cosier atmosphere, Sam climbed into the bed just as the stairs began to creak as Ransom mounted them. However, he didn't immediately enter the bedroom, but went into the bathroom. She heard the shower running, followed by silence as he dried himself. Finally the light clicked off and then he was entering the room, a pile of clothes on one arm and a towel hitched dangerously low around his lean hips.

The clothes were abandoned to the nearest chair, then he ditched the towel just as he climbed into the bed beside her. Sam had the briefest glimpse of tanned skin before the covers blocked out her view. Her heart began to thunder like crazy as he rested on one elbow looking down at her. Emotion closed her throat, and she was ridiculously close to tears, for she loved him so very much, and she had never thought they would be together like this again. She tried to speak, but no words came out. Before she could make another attempt Ransom placed a finger over her lips, sealing them.

'It's late, and we're both tired. Sleep now, Sam. There's always tomorrow,' he said softly, before setting a gentle kiss on her surprised lips, then reaching out to turn off the light. As the room plunged into darkness Sam heard him lie down and make himself comfortable.

She lay staring up at the ceiling, hardly knowing whether to be disappointed or comforted. It was odd that, after pressuring her to join him here, he didn't take advantage of the situation. After a while, though, she knew that, whilst she was vaguely disappointed, she had to admit he was right. She was tired, and there was always tomorrow. Following his example, she made herself comfortable and closed her eyes. Within minutes she was asleep.

Hours later, Sam stirred and winced as sunlight from a crack in the curtain fell across her eyes. She tried to roll away from it, but was brought up short by the body behind her. When she glanced upwards she found smoky grey eyes watching her.

'It's about time you woke up,' Ransom growled, sending shivers down her spine.

She became aware that his hand was slowly stroking up and down her thigh, and deep inside her desire flickered to life. 'What time is it?' she asked, trying to control her breathing, which was turning ragged at that lazy caress.

'Way past kissing time, and more than time to kiss again,' he misquoted, dropping a kiss on her bare shoulder that seared her with its heat.

Sam caught her breath, closing her eyes the better to savour the sensations she hadn't felt for so long. Heart racing, she eased herself onto her back, and the hand that had been on her thigh found its way to her other leg and slipped beneath her nightdress. She reached up to touch his cheek, eyes scanning every centimetre of his beloved face.

'What was stopping you?' she challenged thickly, breath hitching in her throat as his roving hand splayed out across her belly.

'Just the fact that you were asleep. I prefer the woman I'm with to take an active part in the proceedings,' Ransom answered with a wry smile.

Sam's body was rapidly coming to life, and it was all she could do to keep from moving beneath his skilled touch. 'I'm awake now,' she reminded him in little more than a croak.

Flame flared behind his eyes whilst his hand found her breast and his thumb discovered the hardened nipple at its peak. 'You most certainly are,' he murmured huskily as his thumb flickered out, causing her to utter a stifled groan as she arched into the cup of his hand.

She looked at him through sultry eyes. 'Ransom.' His name left her lips on an ache of need, and suddenly they were no longer smiling.

'I know,' he responded tautly. Sitting up, he cast the covers aside and reached for the hem of her nightdress.

Seconds later it was being tossed aside and he took a deep breath as he surveyed the soft curves he had uncovered. 'Beautiful,' he breathed, trailing a path upwards from her thigh to her throat. 'I've been waiting a long time for this,' he added, coming down beside her, his lips hovering tantalisingly close over hers.

Sam slid her arms around him, allowing her hands to rediscover the broad strength of his shoulders. 'The waiting's over,' she told him in scarcely more than a whisper. 'I'm here now, and I'm all yours.'

'Now that's an offer no red-blooded man could refuse,' he breathed, and finally lowered his lips to hers.

It was a kiss that began with the tiniest spark and ended in a conflagration of passion. For Sam, the long-denied hunger broke free of its bounds. She moaned with pleasure as his tongue sought entry to her mouth and began to plunder it with devastating sensuality. Her fingers tightened in his hair as they duelled, stoking the fires that already threatened to burn out of control.

Ransom finally abandoned her mouth, his burning lips tracking a path along the tender curve of her throat. Sam closed her eyes as he travelled lower, and when his mouth found the swollen slope of her breast she caught her breath in an agony of waiting. Then his tongue flickered across the turgid peak and she arched, crying out with pleasure, only to have that pleasure double when his mouth closed on her aching flesh. He nipped and suckled...and sent her senses spinning. Then, when she thought she couldn't take much more, the roller-coaster ride began all over again when he transferred his attention to her other breast.

It was pure delight to be on the receiving end of such tantalising caresses, yet Sam had never been a passive lover. She had to give as well as receive, and when he finally stopped the exquisite torture her hands tangled in his hair and drew his head up.

'My turn,' she commanded, and Ransom allowed her to push him over onto his back, closing his eyes whilst she explored him with hands and lips. It was his turn to moan when she found his flat male nipples and teased them with her teeth, and when her foraging hand encountered the proud shaft of his manhood and closed around it he jumped as if electrified and swore through gritted teeth as he strove to stay in control.

A faint smile of satisfaction curved her lips as she raised her head to look at him. 'Did I hurt you?' she asked, knowing that she hadn't. Far from it.

Ransom took in a hissing breath. 'Hell's teeth! If you want this to last, don't do that again!' he growled.

'OK,' she promised huskily, releasing him, but only to rise to her knees, straddle his hips in one smooth move and take him inside her. As she lowered herself, taking him deeper, Ransom uttered a groan of pleasure and his hands fastened on her hips, holding her still whilst he caught his breath.

'Is that better?' she enquired, whilst her own heart thudded and her body began to clamour for her to move and satisfy the ache of desire that was coiling inside her.

Ransom's lashes fluttered upwards and he looked at her through eyes blazing with barely controlled passion. 'Damn, but I'd forgotten what a tease you can be, Samantha! It's good,' he agreed, then with a nimble movement he rolled, pinning her beneath him. 'But this is better.'

'Mmm, much better.' Sam folded her legs around him, holding him where he was, glorying in his weight and the way he filled her.

Then Ransom moved, and she gasped, fingers clutching at his shoulders at the exquisite sensation. In the beginning his movements were controlled, arousing both of them with tantalising slowness. But the sensations they created, the waves of pleasure that began to roll over them, were too compelling to be denied. He groaned with the effort to remain in control as Sam moved to meet each silken thrust, but need was greater and he couldn't stop himself from thrusting harder and faster.

Sam could sense his control slipping, but she didn't want him to hold back. The coils of desire were tightening and spiralling, taking her higher and higher, and with gasping moans she met his rhythm, egging him on, needing him to take them over the edge. When he finally lost the battle, she held on as he drove on towards release, taking her with him on a gloriously wild ride that ended in a white hot explosion that shattered the senses and catapulted them into a world where pleasure rained like gold dust.

They fell back down to earth with it, exhausted and replete. Sam's eyes stung with tears of joy. This was satisfaction at its most perfect, and she had only ever found it with Ransom—because she loved him. She wanted to hold on to the memory, but even now she could feel sleep creeping over her. When Ransom rolled onto his back, she went with him, snuggling close, one leg over his, an arm curved over his chest. She wanted to speak, tell him how happy she was, but there was no time.

For a second time, sleep claimed her.

CHAPTER NINE

WHEN Sam stirred for the second time, she was alone in the bed. Not that it bothered her at all, for she could hear sounds of movement down below. She stretched and sighed, feeling blissfully relaxed. Making love with Ransom had been like the first time all over again. Although she knew his touch, remembered it vividly, it had still been new and exciting. He had always been a generous lover, and he was the only man who had ever made her feel complete and at peace with herself.

As far as she was concerned, happiness was right here, right now, and a smile as broad as a Cheshire cat's spread across her face.

'Now, what thought brought that look to your face, I wonder?' Ransom enquired teasingly from the doorway, bringing Sam up on an elbow to look at him.

She didn't pretend to misunderstand him. 'I was just thinking,' she replied, allowing her gaze to run lazily over the great expanse of tanned male flesh before her, for Ransom was dressed only in a ragged pair of denim shorts. If there was a sexier view around, she'd eat her hat.

A dangerous glitter entered his grey eyes as he propped himself up against the door jamb. 'I guessed that much. What were you thinking of, or can I guess?'

Sam laughed huskily and held out a hand towards him. 'Come over here and I'll tell you,' she invited.

He shook his head warily. 'Uh-uh. I think I'd better stay here. I don't know as I care for the look in your eyes.'

She dropped her hand and eyed him askance. 'Coward!'

That made him grin. 'Just playing it safe. If I came over

158

there, heaven only knows when we'll surface, and I have something cooking on the stove. We wouldn't want to burn the house down.'

'Not by a real fire, anyway,' Sam conceded wryly, and saw the twinkle of memory in his eyes.

'Things did get kind of heated, didn't they?' he agreed huskily, and Sam sighed reminiscently.

'Oh-h-h, yes.'

Ransom groaned tellingly. 'You're too tempting lying there, and I'm only human. I'm going to go whilst I can. Brunch will be ready in about ten minutes, so get yourself in gear, darling,' he ordered, then disappeared back down the stairs.

Sam sighed ruefully, but then her stomach rumbled loudly, and she realised she was starving. That galvanised her into action, and she hastened from the bed, throwing the covers back to let it air, then gathered up some clothes and headed for the bathroom. Just over ten minutes later she skipped down the stairs dressed in a vest top, shorts and sandals, her damp hair fluffed out about her face to dry in the summer sun.

Ransom was just emptying the contents of a frying pan onto two plates when she walked into the kitchen. He had prepared a full English breakfast and the sight of it made her feel even more ravenous.

'What about my waistline?' she exclaimed as she took a seat at the table. Thankfully she did not need to watch her weight as a rule.

Ransom set the plates down and took his own seat, grinning at her. 'Trust me, there's nothing wrong with your waistline,' he flirted, and when she rewarded him with an old-fashioned look he pointed at her plate. 'Shut up and eat, Samantha. We'll take a long walk later and you'll burn it all off again.'

Sam shut up and ate, enjoying the food although her

heart carried a wistful little ache. Ransom had called her Samantha a few times now, and he had always used to use her full name affectionately. His use of it now was obviously just a hangover from the past, but it was a remembrance of how things had once been.

Later, after they had washed up and tidied the cottage, they went exploring. Ransom appeared to know his way around and she was happy to walk beside him as he took her on a path that followed the stream uphill. It was a glorious afternoon, and there was just enough breeze to cool them as they slowly climbed the valley. When they reached the top a panoramic view opened up before them and Ransom pointed out some of the landmarks.

'We're surrounded by hills here. The Malverns and the Black Mountains of Wales to the west, and the Chilterns to the east. Then there are the Forests of Dean, Wyre and Arden within easy distance. This is a truly beautiful part of the world, Sam.'

She couldn't agree more, and she found a spot where she could sit and lean back against a rock and take in the peace. 'Will you retire to this area one day? I always thought you would be near the sea.'

Ransom came to join her. 'The Severn is only a few miles away, and the Bristol channel, so it wouldn't be far. I'm hoping to persuade Simon to sell me the cottage, but he's resisting.'

'You come here quite a lot, then?'

'Whenever I need the peace and quiet to think,' he told her, drawing up his knees and resting his arms on them. 'I first came here six years ago, and the last time was only the other day.'

That piece of news was something of a jolt to Sam's heart. To think of him needing peace and quiet as recently as that was disquieting. 'I imagined you stayed in London.'

Ransom kept his gaze on the view as he answered. 'I did

to begin with, but it's impossible to think in the city, so I came here. That was when I began to see things clearly and came to terms with everything that's happened, then and now,' he went on casually, as if their conversation were not about a sore subject.

Sam shifted uncomfortably. She had never been able to entirely rid herself of guilt over what she had done. 'I see. Well, you couldn't have come to a more peaceful spot. I'm glad it helped,' she said sincerely, and he turned his head to look at her.

'It certainly got me thinking straight,' he agreed, smiling faintly. 'Once I got to thinking rationally, a lot became clear. One thing didn't change. I still wanted to throttle you.'

Sam sighed heavily. 'I'm sorry,' she apologised yet again, and Ransom quirked an eyebrow questioningly.

'What for, exactly?'

She shrugged helplessly. 'For everything. For misleading you.'

Ransom shook his head and laughed softly. 'Misleading me. Now that's a very apposite phrase. Reminds me of magic tricks and misdirection. And do you know what the really funny thing is? As a boy, I always saw through them. Just goes to show you what a dollop of emotion can do,' he added, more to himself than to her.

Sam frowned, trying to follow what he was saying. 'I'm not sure I understand you,' she said, and that caused him to laugh dryly.

'I'm pretty sure you don't, but don't let it bother you,' he advised her, leaning back against the rock and stretching out his long tanned legs beside hers. Reaching for her arm, he urged her backwards and round so that she was lying across his lap looking up at him. He traced the line of her mouth with a gentle finger.

'What made you come back? Why didn't you stay in Italy?' he wanted to know, and her heart clenched.

As if there were any doubt! She had missed him, and maybe in the back of her mind he had drawn her back because England was where he was. None of which she could tell him. 'I missed chips. They only have French fries abroad,' she invented, her lips tingling where his finger had touched.

He rakish grin appeared. 'So, we owe your return to the fish and chip shops of old England, do we?'

Sam laughed softly. 'That and a few other things. It's too long a list to bore you with now.'

'If there's one thing I remember about you, darling, it's that you're rarely if ever boring,' Ransom corrected, and his gaze centred on her mouth. 'Intoxicating. Alluring,' he went on, punctuating the words with tantalisingly brief kisses. 'Now, they sound more like it.'

Sam tried to cling onto the last kiss, but he raised his head, and she was left looking up at him longingly. 'Are you trying to seduce me?' she asked softly, feeling her blood pulsing thickly through her veins.

He smiled, but there was heat in his eyes. 'It didn't escape me that we're all alone out here, with nothing but time on our hands. A little seduction might not go amiss. How am I doing?' This last question was accompanied by the slow trail of his hand from her face to her breast, which he cupped, and he started to trace lazy circles around her nipple with his thumb.

It was uncanny that he only had to touch her and her bones started to melt. 'You're doing all right,' she answered with a tiny gasp as pleasure darted through her, bringing life to the smouldering embers of desire.

There was a wolfish gleam in his eyes. 'You don't think that after six years I might be losing my touch?'

'Not a chance,' she denied huskily. 'Are you going to keep talking or kiss me again?'

'All good things come to she who waits,' he countered with a smile and she narrowed her eyes at him.

'Ransom!'

'Yes, Sam?' he returned mildly, and she could feel the laughter in him.

She punched him on the shoulder. 'You're a rogue, do you know that?'

He shrugged. 'I've been accused of many things over the years.'

'Well, if you don't want to be accused of being a rotten tease, you'd better kiss me right now,' Sam commanded, grabbing a handful of his tee shirt and tugging his head down towards hers.

'Hey! There's no need to be ro—' Ransom began to protest laughingly, only to have the words cut off as Sam reached up to close the gap and put an end to his teasing by kissing him.

Talking immediately became surplus to requirements. All they needed to know was conveyed by touch. Each sensual kiss was surpassed by the next as they engaged in an erotic duel as old as time itself. Desire was a tinder-dry forest just waiting for the spark that would ignite it. Every nip of teeth or brush of tongue brought them closer to the point where conflagration was inevitable—and necessary. Only the need for air finally made them pause at the very brink.

Ransom dragged his mouth away, resting his forehead against hers as they gasped in ragged lungfuls of oxygen. Sam groaned and closed her eyes, trying desperately to steady her breathing. She wanted nothing more than to make love with him, and knew he wanted the same from his unmistakable sign of arousal. It was like a particularly cruel form of torture to get so close, then have to stop.

Then she felt the brush of air on her face as Ransom

laughed unevenly. 'We'd better stop before we set the whole place alight. They haven't had any rain hereabouts for a while,' he joked tautly.

She groaned again. 'I'll risk it if you will,' she offered, slipping her hands under the edge of his tee shirt and running them over the firm planes of his back.

It was Ransom's turn to groan. 'That's one hell of a tempting offer, but we have to be sensible. Besides, I have a much better idea.'

Sam pulled away so that she could see him without going cross-eyed. 'You do?'

His eyes darted flame as he nodded. 'Have you seen the size of that bath?'

Instantly erotic pictures flashed into her mind, and that ache she had been striving to ignore began to swell. 'It's big,' she agreed thickly.

Ransom grinned. 'It certainly is, and we'll both be hot and dusty when we get back to the cottage.'

Sam's hand paused in the small of his back. 'I like the way your mind works, Mr Shaw,' she said, sitting up.

'Thought you might,' he growled sexily as he rose and held out a hand to help her to her feet.

Sam fully expected him to release her hand, but he didn't, he kept hold of it as he headed off round the side of the hill. 'Why aren't we going back the same way?' she wanted to know, and he grinned down at her.

'Because although this route is longer, it's less tiring. We don't want to be too exhausted to enjoy ourselves, do we?'

She couldn't argue with that. 'You have an answer to everything, don't you?'

Something strange flickered across his face momentarily, then vanished before she could grasp what it was. 'I do, and it's about time you realised it. But you know what they say, better late than never!' Ransom responded mockingly, and Sam blinked in surprise.

She didn't know what to make of that. It sounded like a criticism, but how it applied to herself she had no idea. She puzzled over it for some time, until they reached a steep area, and negotiating it safely sent the thought from her mind. It would be many days before it returned.

A few hours later Sam lay back in the bath with a sigh of satisfaction. Making love in the king-size bath had been an experience she wouldn't forget in a hurry. They had created quite a storm, in more ways than one, and she had just been busily spreading towels over the floor to mop up the over-flow.

Settled comfortably, she raised her arms from the water and examined her hands. 'My fingers are looking like prunes,' she observed mildly.

'Let me see,' Ransom commanded from behind her, reaching around to take her wrist and examine the wrinkles on her fingers. 'Mmm, we've probably been in here too long.' His chin brushed her hair as he spoke.

'Probably,' she agreed lazily, twining her fingers through his. 'Funnily enough, time wasn't the main thing on my mind.'

'I wonder why,' Ransom teased, running his free hand caressingly down the curves of her body as far as he could reach.

Sam caught hold of it before it could wreak too much havoc with her senses. 'I wouldn't do that unless you're prepared to take the consequences,' she warned flirta-tiously, and felt rather than heard him laugh.

'What consequences would they be?'

She smiled to herself, totally and blissfully relaxed. 'Oh, I'll think of something appropriate.'

He laughed aloud. 'I have every confidence that you will,

Sam, darling. In fact, I'm banking on it,' he added, nipping at her ear and sending delicious tingles through her body.

'I don't think you should rush it, Ransom. After all, you're not as young as you were!' she warned with a giggle.

'Now that sounds like you're casting aspersions on my virility. Not a wise thing to do at any time. I might just have to prove to you just how wrong you are,' he growled back.

'Promises, promises.'

'I wouldn't wave any more red rags, Samantha. The only thing stopping me from action is the thought of causing further damage to the floor.'

Sam winced, biting her lip in concern. 'Do you think it will be OK?'

'Well, I'm pretty sure we won't end up in the kitchen by the direct route,' he responded dryly. 'But maybe we'd be more comfortable in the other room. Pull out the plug, Sam.'

She sat up and reached for the chain whilst Ransom rose and climbed out of the bath. There were fluffy towelling robes hanging on the door, and he put one on and held out the other for her to slip into after she climbed out of the bath. Then he swept her up in his arms and carried her through to the bedroom. He was just about to set her down on the bed when Sam's stomach gave an audible growl of protest. He paused.

'We haven't eaten since brunch,' she reminded him with a winsome smile.

'Meaning you want feeding, I suppose,' Ransom returned sardonically.

Sam batted her eyelashes at him. 'I'll make it worth your while,' she promised with a provocative sideways look.

Ransom laughed and let her go, so that she dropped to

the bed with a squeal of surprise and bounced once before she could steady herself.

'Hey!' she protested, but he merely grinned unrepentantly and walked out of the room.

Sam sighed and lay back, staring up at the ceiling, a silly smile on her face. She sighed happily. This was how it had been between them six years ago, and she had missed the gentle banter and ultimate togetherness. Of course, she knew it wasn't going to last, but just for a while she was going to bask in the glow of it.

She heard Ransom moving about downstairs, then the stairs creaking as he mounted them, and sat up, propping the pillows up against the headboard and making herself comfortable. He walked in with a tray, which he set down on the bed, then settled himself beside her.

'Cheese, crackers, tomatoes, cold chicken and a nicely chilled bottle of Chardonnay.' He pointed out the goodies he had found, then poured two glasses of wine and handed her one.

Sam sipped it. 'Hmm, delicious,' she proclaimed and took a piece of chicken in her other hand, biting into it with relish.

By the time their stomachs were satisfied, they had polished off most of what Ransom had brought upstairs. He topped up their glasses, pushed the tray to the foot of the bed, stretched out comfortably and pulled Sam into his side.

She rested her head against his shoulder, and could hear the solid beat of his heart. He had always made her feel safe—as if nothing could ever hurt her. Ironically, when she had been hurt, it had been because of him, not by him.

'I could stay like this for ever.' She sighed, breathing in the distinctive male scent of him, trying to hold it in her memory.

'I know what you mean,' Ransom responded. 'Unfortunately, I'm due in court on Monday.'

Sam groaned. 'I don't want to think about Monday and work,' she protested, although what she really didn't want to think about was the weekend and their time together being over. Not yet. Not until the last minute, anyway.

'OK, let's talk about something else,' he said easily, setting his glass down on the bedside table and folding his arms around her. 'Tell me about your family.'

'My family?' That was the last thing she had expected him to say. What on earth did he want to know about her family for? He was hardly likely to meet any of them. They didn't have that sort of a relationship.

'Um-hmm. You once told me it was a large one. How many of you are there?' he asked idly, and Sam took a careful sip of wine, thinking fast. The question was a reasonable one, given what she herself had said, and it was hardly a taboo subject.

'To be honest there aren't that many in my particular family,' she told him with a smile coming to her lips the way it always did when she thought of them. 'There are my parents. As you know, my father is half Italian, making the rest of us a quarter Italian. It's enough to keep the emotional fires bubbling away, ready to overflow at the least little thing.'

'Sounds highly entertaining!'

Sam chuckled, warming to her theme. 'Believe me, there isn't a minute when something isn't happening. Yet it makes us close. Even the arguments, when they're over, make the bond even stronger. I have two brothers and two sisters.'

'All married?' Ransom queried idly, and she shook her head.

'Tony's the only one who's never been married,' she corrected him. 'I was the eldest daughter.'

'Was that hard?' Ransom asked curiously, but Sam shrugged dismissively.

'No more than it is for the oldest siblings in any family. I was like an extra parent to my brothers and sisters, but I never minded. It's just the way it is,' she added simply.

'You take your responsibility to your family very seriously, don't you?' Ransom mused.

'Of course! We're family!' There was nothing more to be said.

'Sounds to me as if any one of you would do anything to help one of the others if they were in trouble,' Ransom reasoned, brushing his cheek over her hair in a gentle caress.

'In an instant. We wouldn't even have to think about it. Not that it happens often,' she hastened to add. In fact, the last time had been six years ago.

Behind her, Ransom looked thoughtful. 'It must be impossible to sit and watch a family member in trouble without wanting to do something.'

Sam sat up and looked at him. 'Oh, it is. But if you have the means to do something to help, you do it. No question!' she declared fervently, waving her glass around as she did so.

Ransom smiled, but there was a considering look in his eyes. 'You look like a lioness preparing to protect her cubs at all costs,' he said, taking the glass from her before she spilt its contents over the bed.

'There's nothing wrong in that,' she pointed out swiftly. 'When the people I care about are in trouble, I'll do whatever I have to do to help them,' she declared adamantly.

'A noble idea, Sam, darling, but who looks out for you?' Ransom tipped his head on one side queryingly.

She waved that away. 'I can look out for myself, so that isn't important.'

'Really? You don't think that someone might consider it vitally important?' he countered mildly, causing her to frown.

'Why would they?' she asked and he laughed ruefully.

'Maybe because they feel as strongly as you do,' he offered up, and Sam blinked, sitting back on her heels.

'I never considered that,' she confessed, frowning heavily.

Ransom looked at her steadily and shook his head. 'No. You didn't. Your heart's in the right place, Sam, but your judgement sometimes stinks.'

Her eyes widened in affront. 'Hey, I resent that!'

All he did was raise his eyebrows at her. 'Resent away, but the truth's the truth. Anyway, let's not fight over it. Tell me about your life in Italy.'

Sam stared at him as alarm bells went off in her head. Suddenly she was back in the middle of that minefield. Italy and the details of her time there were not open for discussion. 'There's nothing to tell,' she told him with finality, and Ransom smiled ruefully.

'Was I getting to sound as if I was in a courtroom?'

Relaxing, now that she had stemmed the flow of questions, Sam grinned. 'Just a little.'

Ransom sat up and cupped her chin with his hand. 'Sorry about that. However, you've given me an interesting insight into how your mind works. You'd go into battle at the drop of a hat, wouldn't you?'

'I don't go to such trouble for everyone,' she pointed out teasingly.

'Don't worry, I get the picture,' Ransom assured her, giving her a long, hard look. 'You only go to such lengths for those you care about. Which means,' he went on in a wry voice, 'that I won't be given the treatment. Seeing as our relationship is purely physical.'

Sam's breath hitched in her throat and her stomach twisted into an uncomfortable knot. 'That's right,' she lied without batting an eyelid. 'Although I would take you to the hospital if you did yourself a serious injury.'

His lips twitched. 'That's a comforting thought.'

Sam smiled faintly in return. 'I'd do as much for a stray dog,' she added helpfully, taking his hand from her chin and holding it, palm upwards. 'If I could read palms, I could probably tell you if you had a long lifeline.' With one finger she traced the various lines she could see.

'I have no plans to pop my clogs for some time yet,' he replied with heavy irony, and she shot him a winsome smile from beneath her lashes.

'Good, because I have plans.'

One eyebrow quirked. 'Plans?'

'Mmm-hmm. I don't want to talk about me any more. I want to concentrate on you.' Letting go of his hand, Sam scrambled off the bed and removed the tray, setting it on the floor by the door.

'Need any help?' Ransom enquired, watching her with a gleam of interest in his eyes.

Sam returned to the bed and sat on her knees beside him. 'I can manage. All you need to do is lie down and relax,' she responded, pushing him down until he lay flat on his back. Then her nimble fingers began to untie the belt of his robe.

Ransom took a deep breath. 'Relaxing might not be possible,' he pointed out as she took the edges of the robe and pushed them to the side.

She surveyed the sight of the tanned male body spread out before her and bit her lip to hide a wicked grin. 'Hmm,' she giggled softly. 'I think you're getting ahead of me,' she said, tracing her fingers downwards from his neck to his stomach, which jerked under her touch.

With a groan, Ransom covered his eyes with his arm. 'It's called…anticipation,' he gritted out, breath hissing in as her hand found him and began to stroke gently.

Sam could feel her own body turning molten inside at the sight of him laid out at her mercy. Swiftly she released him and shrugged out of her own robe, tossing it to the floor. Then she bent over him, hands and lips tracing the undulating planes of his chest, teasing his flat male nipples until he moaned, then she moved back downwards towards her ultimate goal.

She didn't reach it. Ransom, pushed almost to the limit, prevented the sweet torture she had planned by taking a handful of her hair and gently pulling her head up. When their eyes locked, hers were smouldering but his were ablaze.

'My turn,' he declared, pushing her onto her back and wreaking delicious havoc on her already inflamed senses.

He started with her breasts, which were already engorged and aching for his touch. When his mouth closed on one turgid nipple Sam thrashed and moaned, fingers clutching onto the sheet as her body arched upwards, wanting more. Devilishly, he took his time, abandoning her breast only to lay siege to its mate. He drove her towards the edge of insanity with his teasing, but finally he retreated, and Sam closed her eyes, listening to her thudding heart as she felt his mouth and hands trailing across her belly…then lower. Finally his hand slipped between her thighs, and she was so ready for him that a whimper of need broke from her taut throat. He stroked and caressed her, tightening the throbbing, spiralling coils of need until she was ready to scream…and then he lowered his head and used his lips and tongue to send her toppling over the edge into a sizzling climax.

When her breathing returned to normal she found Ransom had moved so that his body was resting over hers, his weight on his elbows as he watched her.

'Was that what you had in mind?' he asked gruffly, sampling her lips with butterfly kisses.

'You'll never know now, will you?' she responded

faintly, then caught her breath as he moved, sheathing himself inside her in one easy action.

Very slowly Ransom began to move, and Sam, who had thought her shattered senses would need time to recover, could feel her body responding to the stimulus of his. He knew her so well. Knew what she needed, knew what she craved. Sam met his rhythm and matched it, moving with him, taking them both on that crazy roller-coaster ride. Yet there came a point when their mutual need for release overwhelmed their sensual lovemaking. The tempo increased, and, though he strove to maintain it, Ransom's control shattered. With all restraint gone, Sam held on tight as he drove into her, sending them careering over the edge into another white-hot climax.

Before their shattered bodies slipped into unconsciousness, Ransom eased himself off Sam and she sighed, following him to tuck herself close to his side. He folded his arms around her and stared up at the ceiling. Sleep was calling but he fended it off, for he had a great deal to think about that night.

CHAPTER TEN

LATE Sunday evening Ransom parked his car before Sam's flat and switched off the engine. It had been a magical few days, perfect in almost every way, and was over far too soon for Sam. She felt a lump of emotion rise to clog her throat as she knew the weekend, and this extra time with Ransom, was almost over. Instinctively she attempted to hold back the moment of parting.

'Would you like to come in for coffee?' she asked him hopefully, thinking that perhaps she could steal one more night.

However, Ransom glanced at the clock on the dashboard and shook his head. 'Can't I'm afraid. The time's getting on, and, like I said, I have to be in court tomorrow.'

She had half hoped he would say something like: Another time, perhaps, but he didn't, and she had to swallow her disappointment. 'It wouldn't look good if you fell asleep at the bar!' she managed to tease with a small smile.

Ransom pulled a face. 'Definitely not with this presiding judge. He eats QCs for breakfast.'

Sam laughed as he expected her to. 'We wouldn't want that. Are you prosecuting or defending?'

'Defending,' he elaborated, reaching out to tuck a stray hair behind her ear.

'You'll win the case,' she told him confidently, causing his lips to twitch.

'You know this because…?'

She looked at him solemnly, meaning what she said and wanting him to know that, at least. 'You're good at what you do. No question about it.'

Ransom scratched the bridge of his nose with his thumb, looking faintly quizzical. 'Thank you for the compliment.'

'You're welcome.'

Silence fell between them, and Sam knew in her heart that the moment had finally come. He was about to go his way and she hers. Because she felt like howling, she made herself be upbeat.

'So, do you think this weekend has done the trick?' she asked directly, and though it was too dark to see the look in his eyes, she thought they glinted.

'I'm certainly hoping so,' Ransom responded evenly, and she nodded.

'Good.'

'OK, then,' he said, slapping his hands together. 'Let's get your case from the boot and I'll see you inside,' he proposed, climbing out.

'You don't have to do that,' Sam protested as she too got out.

Ransom collected her case from the boot and set the alarm. 'I was raised to be a gentleman, and, whilst I might fall short in some ways, I always walk a lady to her door.'

Not only did he walk her to her door, but he took her key from her, opened the door, turned on the light and set her case inside before returning the key to her. 'There you are. All safe and sound.'

Sam closed her fingers around the cold metal, ice in her heart and lead in her stomach. 'I hate long goodbyes. Let's make this short and sweet, shall we?'

Ransom's lips twisted into a wry smile. 'In that case, what about one last kiss, for old time's sake?' he suggested, taking a step towards her and taking her into his arms. Sam slipped her hands around his neck and looked up at him seriously.

'We had some fun, didn't we?'

His eyes took on a strange gleam. 'We surely did, but

all good things have to come to an end. All that remains is this…' he added as he lowered his head and their lips met.

Sam had intended to keep it light, but, with the prospect of this being the last kiss they would ever share, instinct took over and she put her heart and soul into it. Not to stir passion, but to give him with her kiss what she could never tell him—that she loved him and always would.

Finally, trembling, she broke away, tried to smile, but failed miserably. Emotion choked her throat and all she could say was a gruff: 'Goodbye!' and retreat into her flat, locking the door behind her.

Left outside, Ransom shook his head. He ran a trembling hand through his hair and turned to stare at the closed door with eyes that glittered with volatile emotions. Then shutters came down, and his mouth set in a determined line as he walked away without a word.

Standing on the other side of the door, Sam heard his footsteps fade away and felt—nothing. She was strangely numb, and supposed it was because she had gone through this before. This time it was expected, so she was clearly handling it better. Having known from the start that the relationship was going to be short and sweet, she had no shock to contend with. Which was good, for there was no point crying for something that couldn't be changed.

Of course, she was only fooling herself. The feeling lasted until she climbed into bed, but then the absence of his body beside her hit home. The flood wall disintegrated and, not for the first time, she cried herself to sleep.

In the morning she felt drained but knew there was nothing to be gained from moping in bed, so she got up, made herself eat some toast and went to work. The routine helped in the following days, for the hotel was so busy, there was little or no time to think. She welcomed the fact that she was exhausted when she got home, for it meant she fell asleep almost the instant her head hit the pillow.

By Thursday she was resigned to waiting for time to paper over the cracks again. Time was something she had plenty of. In the meantime, spring came around early. She cleaned out cupboards, washed down walls. Generally did all those little jobs that she had mentally put aside for later.

That evening she was intending to vacuum the three-piece suite, and had the cushions off and was busily searching the cracks for things she had lost when the front doorbell went. Wondering who it could be, Sam clambered to her feet and went to answer its call. The bell went again before she had reached the door, and she frowned.

'All right! All right!' she muttered under her breath, promising that if it was someone selling something, they were going to get short shrift. Jerking open the door, she was about to say something really pithy when she saw who it was. 'Ransom?' she queried in astonishment, blinking to make sure her imagination hadn't conjured him up. He was still there, dressed casually in jeans, shirt and trainers, looking incredibly handsome, and she was completely thrown. 'What are you doing here? I didn't expect to see you!'

That declaration brought a tight smile to his lips. 'I'm sure you didn't,' he said grimly.

His tone had her nerves skittering without knowing why. 'I...er...why aren't you at home preparing for court?'

'The case was adjourned,' he explained tersely. 'It gave me the opportunity to get some other important business done. Then I came to see you. Are you going to invite me in?' Automatically Sam stepped back and Ransom walked inside. Shutting the door, she followed him into her lounge, which must have looked to him as if a bomb had hit it. Not that that registered. All she could think was that something was up, or else why would he be here?

'What's happened? Is everything all right?' She shot rapid questions at his back.

With an odd-sounding laugh he turned to face her, arms

crossed in what her mind fancifully dubbed battle position. 'Why would you assume there's something wrong?'

Sam quickly realised she might have been a bit hasty, jumping to conclusions, and attempted to cover her confusion by picking up the cushions and restoring them to the settee. 'Well, you're here, and…'

'You couldn't think of any other reason why I might be here?' Ransom finished for her, and she straightened up, still clutching one of the cushions.

'Actually…no.'

Shaking his head, Ransom laughed again, but Sam didn't feel there was a great deal of amusement in it. 'No. You're always so certain, aren't you, Sam?'

She had no idea where this was going. 'About some things, yes,' she agreed warily, frowning as she watched him walk over to the nearest window, hold back the net and look out for a moment.

Finally he dropped the curtain and turned, slipping his hands into his trouser pockets in a casual gesture that was belied by the stern look on his face. 'Tell me something, Sam. What do you think last weekend was all about?'

Now that question took her completely by surprise. Her jaw dropped and she stared at him rather stupidly. 'Last weekend?' Why was he asking? Surely he knew? The answer was as plain as the nose on his face.

Ransom nodded. 'Take your time. Just tell me in your own words what you think last weekend was all about,' he repeated, sounding to Sam just as if he were interrogating a witness, and she didn't like it one bit.

'This is my home, Ransom, not a courtroom, so don't try your clever tactics on me,' she reminded him, tossing the cushion onto the settee and folding her arms. 'Anyway, you know the answer to your question as well as I do. Last weekend was about sex. We found we were still attracted to each other, so we decided to do something about it. We went away and we went to bed together, and now we're getting on with our lives,' she declared, chin raised at a belligerent angle, annoyed that he was making her say it.

Ransom rocked back on his heels and looked at her consideringly. 'Is that so? You really think that's why I went away with you?' he challenged and she went still, eyes narrowing. What was he playing at?

'I don't think, I know,' she said firmly.

In response to that Ransom sauntered a few steps closer. 'Do you always know what everyone is thinking and feeling?'

Sam drew in an irritated breath, feeling rather like a fish on a hook. 'In some instances, yes,' she declared, throwing up her hands. 'What is this all about?'

Those fascinating grey eyes suddenly flashed sparks in her direction. 'OK, I'll tell you what it's all about, Samantha, darling. It's about this one very important point. Has it never occurred to you that you might have it all wrong?' he demanded to know in a voice that finally revealed a smouldering wealth of pent-up emotion.

She was stunned; her mouth formed an O of surprise. 'You're angry.' It was a feeble thing to say in view of the waves coming from him, and got a suitable answer.

'Oh-h-h, no, darling. I'm not angry. I'm furious!' he corrected, pacing about the room like a caged tiger, then swinging to face her again. 'There have been times in these last few days that I have felt like committing murder. In fact, if I didn't love you as much as I do, I'd cheerfully throttle you right here and now!'

Sam was so bemused by the waves of anger washing over her that it took a few seconds for what he'd actually said to sink in. 'What did you say?' she asked faintly, convinced she must have heard wrong.

'I said I could cheerfully throttle you,' Ransom obliged, and Sam closed her eyes.

'I got that part. I meant the other bit. You said...' She swallowed to moisten a suddenly dry mouth. 'You said... At least, I think you said...'

Ransom laughed wryly. 'Now she shows signs of doubt! I said I love you, Sam. Always have, always will,' he repeated shortly, not sounding exactly loving, but under the circumstances that was understandable.

The strength went out of her legs and she sat down in a hurry. Dazed, Sam pressed her hands to her cheeks. 'You can't do!' she argued in a strangled voice.

He spread his hands. 'Is there a law I haven't come across that says Ransom Shaw isn't allowed to love Samantha Grimaldi?'

She swallowed hard, still not prepared to believe what he was saying because of what it would mean. 'No, no! You stopped loving me six years ago!'

Ransom smiled tightly and shook his head. 'Correction. Six years ago I hated you for a long while. I never actually stopped loving you. So, you see, your plan only half worked.'

Her heart lurched at those last telling words. 'My...plan?' How could he possibly know about that? The answer was like a lead weight in her stomach.

Grim amusement lit up his eyes. 'Smoke and mirrors, Sam. The old magician's trick of misdirection. Only, instead of making me look somewhere else, your plan was to make me angry so that I wouldn't look at all!'

By this time Sam's heart was thudding so loudly, she wouldn't have been surprised if he could hear it. 'W-why would I do such a thing?' she stammered, wondering how on earth he knew so much. It wasn't possible. She had been so careful.

He had the answer. 'The very question I asked myself just recently when I stopped thinking with my heart and started to use my brain again,' he told her, eyes not leaving her stricken face. 'Why would you do it? The answer, when it came to me, was really very simple. You'd do it to protect me, because you loved me. The way you instinctively protect those you care about.'

Sam's colour fluctuated at this further proof of the depth of his understanding. 'To protect you from what?' she croaked, unable to take in that this was really happening.

'That I didn't know, but, for whatever reason, you loved me enough to try to heal the wound you had made,' Ransom returned confidently.

She made an effort to concentrate, for this was vitally important. 'Let me get this straight. Even though I told you I didn't, you think I loved you?' she challenged, and a gleam appeared in his eyes.

'Uh-uh. To quote your own phrase, I don't think, I know. Despite what you told me, you loved me six years ago, and, more importantly, you love me still.'

His percipience took her breath away. 'I do?' she charged faintly, and he nodded.

'Without a shadow of a doubt,' he declared firmly. 'So, my darling, would you care to revise what you think you know?'

She closed her eyes as the enormity of what he was saying hit home. What he was saying gave the lie to everything she had believed these last six years. *She had got it all wrong.* Her plan had never completely worked! Ransom had never stopped loving her! As for her assumptions... She had thought he would hate her, but he didn't. She had been sure he couldn't love her, but he did. More than that. He knew she loved him. Was absolutely certain of it, because he had worked out that she had lied. Lied because she loved him.

Opening her eyes at last, she looked at him helplessly. 'How?' she whispered, horrified.

Ransom released a pent-up breath. 'How did I work it

out? Rather late in the day—six years late, actually, I started to think again. You had me fooled for a long time, and that isn't an easy thing to do. But the weekends we spent together opened my eyes. Everything I learned about you didn't gel with the woman who dumped me. Looking back, I could see that you literally changed from one day to the next. Nobody does that without a reason. Realising that, I suddenly knew what the reason was. Love.'

Sam's lips began to tremble, and she stared hard at the ceiling, trying to hold back tears. It had hurt her so much to hurt him, and now she realised it had all been for nothing. 'What do you want me to tell you?' she asked brokenly.

'The truth would be nice,' he invited with gentle mockery. 'Don't I deserve it? For sheer, dogged persistence at least?'

Sam knew there was no point in keeping up the lie now. A growing lump of emotion threatened to block her throat, and she had to swallow hard in order to speak. 'You're right. I did love you, Ransom,' she confessed thickly. 'I still do,' she added, tears welling up in her eyes and overflowing, running unchecked down her cheeks.

Any remaining tension and anger drained out of him in an instant, and the expression of relief on his face told its own story. 'That's all I need to know for now,' he said gruffly as he closed the gap between them and drew her up into his arms, wrapping them around her tightly as if afraid she might yet vanish again.

Sam held on too, her fingers fastening onto handfuls of his shirt, and as she stood within the shelter of his arms she finally accepted the fact that his feelings for her were as deep and abiding as they had ever been. Even in her wildest dreams she had never thought he would ever tell her he loved her again. Now he had, several times, and her heart began to fill with the unexpected joy of it. Ransom loved her. It was incredible yet true.

'You really still love me?' She just had to ask again.

'I really do,' Ransom responded firmly, and the protective walls she had built up around her heart gave way, all her love for him pouring forth, filling her with an unbounded happiness.

'Oh, God, I love you so much!' she told him, heart twisting at the irony that it had taken her six years to rediscover something that had never been lost. Which was why it was vitally important that she keep telling him she loved him, after hiding it for so long.

'I know,' he said thickly, and kissed her.

It was not a kiss designed to arouse passion, but to convey a depth of feeling that mere words could never do. It was a commitment, a promise…a whole host of things, but primarily it was a declaration of love.

When Ransom drew his lips from hers, Sam gazed up into his eyes, knowing that she owed him an explanation for her actions. 'I'm so sorry I lied, but, you have to believe me, it was for the best of reasons,' she apologised.

'Was it? It certainly didn't feel that way to me,' he countered, but though she winced she held his gaze.

'Yes, it was,' she insisted, chewing her lip because of what she had to say. 'There are things you don't know, things I can't tell you, even now,' she declared huskily.

'Can't or won't?' he asked hardily, and she swallowed, licking her lips nervously.

'Can't and won't,' she replied, staring into his eyes, trying her best to make him understand that she was not playing games now. 'I swore an oath not to tell, and, heaven help me, even if it drives a wedge between us, I cannot go back on my word!'

Much to her surprise, Ransom nodded slowly. 'I see. In that case, let me tell you what I know, Sam,' he declared quietly. His confidence was almost scary, but this time she was prepared to argue.

'I don't see how you could know anything,' she charged faintly.

'Reg Dunne.'

She was totally thrown by that. 'Reg Dunne?' The name meant absolutely nothing.

'Reg is the man I hired to find out some facts about six years ago. He was able to tell me that you had a brother who worked for Grimaldi, and that between the day that you broke with me, and the announcement of your engagement, he was shipped out of the country. He was also able to discover that this brother had a gambling problem. Not much, but it made perfect sense to me. Your brother was in debt. He took money he had no right to, and, in order to cover it up and save your family from ruin, you agreed to marry Leno Grimaldi. How am I doing so far?'

That he had been able to piece so much together from so little was a shock. Yet it made no difference. 'I can't answer that,' she informed him in a hushed voice, willing him to understand. To say yes or no would be to break her oath. Her throat worked madly. 'God knows, I don't want to lose you again, but if it comes as a choice between you and my word, then there is no choice. Don't make me choose. Please don't,' she pleaded, pulling herself away from him and rubbing her hands up and down her arms anxiously.

Ransom caught her by the shoulders and compelled her to look at him. 'It's OK, Sam,' he said gently. 'I won't make you choose, because I think I understand what went on back then. I believe I'm close to the truth, and it makes me wish I could have helped you. I wasn't in a position to, was I?'

Sam's lips twisted into a rueful smile. 'You know I can't answer that either.'

Ransom went still, then with a sigh he pulled her back into his arms. 'You just have, sweetheart, in a roundabout way. Don't worry,' he added, when she tensed. 'Your oath is unbroken.'

A lump lodged itself in her throat, for he had just proved he trusted her without needing to be told anything more. 'Giving you up was the hardest thing I've ever done. I thought, if I could make you hate me, you'd move on. I didn't want to hurt you, but...' she began, only to stop when he placed a finger on her lips.

'I know you acted with the best of intentions, and that you hurt yourself as much as me, but if you ever, ever do anything like it again... Well, I might not be responsible for what would happen,' Ransom declared wryly.

Her heart leapt, then galloped on at a faster pace as she looked up into suddenly dancing grey eyes. 'You make it sound as if we have a future.'

One eyebrow lifted challengingly. 'What makes you think we don't?'

Sam bit her lip. She wanted to believe there was hope now, but it was hard after all she had done. 'How can you forgive me so easily?'

He laughed softly, teasingly. 'Because I love you. Besides, I lied to you too.'

That surprised her. 'You did?'

He had the grace to look a little shamefaced. 'When I said I didn't care about you. That what I wanted from you was sex. All lies, because I needed to find out how you felt about me first. After all, the first time I asked you to marry me, you threw the offer back in my face,' Ransom informed her in a faintly taunting tone.

Not that it mattered to Sam. She had picked out the salient point. 'Are you planning to ask me again?'

The wolfish look returned to his grey eyes. 'It had occurred to me.'

Feeling faintly euphoric, Sam leant her head on his shoulder. 'I might even say yes, if you explain about last weekend. If it wasn't about sex, why did you rush me into bed?'

Ransom's soft laughter was aimed at himself. 'If I rushed you into bed, it was because I'd waited so long for you, I couldn't wait any longer,' he admitted, then sighed. 'When I saw you again at the Hunts', I was stunned by the strength of my feelings for you, and my first instinct was to protect myself. After all, if you were the sort of woman I believed you to be, I couldn't let you discover how I felt.'

Sam slipped a hand around his neck, her thumb gently caressing his skin. 'I can understand that.'

Ransom dropped a kiss on her hair. 'Anyway, I covered my tracks, and soon realised you weren't after Alex. Then the other things I discovered about you in Norfolk set me thinking. If you did what you did out of love, you might still love me. If that were true, then I was determined to get you back by hook or by crook.'

She glanced up at him through narrowed eyes. 'That wasn't the impression you gave me!' she said accusingly, and he shrugged.

'I told you all was fair in love and war, and this was love for me. That was what last weekend was all about. Not what you thought, a good dose of uninhibited sex, then thank you and goodbye. I wanted answers, and I got them.'

Her eyes widened as realisation dawned. 'So that was why you asked so many questions? My God, you're devious!'

'And you're not, which makes an ideal combination,' he countered with a roguish smile. 'Anyway, the upshot was, I left you cooling your heels whilst I made some enquiries. Then I came to see you.'

Now that she understood, Sam was able to smile at the memory. 'You were like an angry bull, breathing fury!'

Ransom cupped her head with his hands, looking deeply into her eyes. 'I was furious that you hadn't come to me. That really hurt, because I needed to be able to help you, too. OK, so I know now that there was nothing I could do, but that was a special case. You've got to promise me, Sam, that if anything serious happens again, you'll talk to me about it. There isn't anything we can't work out together.'

'I promise.'

A slow smile curved his lips. 'So, will you marry me at the second time of asking?'

Sam glanced up at him from under her lashes. 'Will you give me some time to think about it?'

Ransom shook his head in swift refusal. 'Listen, darling, it's taken me six years to get to ask you again, and I don't intend to wait a second longer than I have to for your answer. So, what's it to be, yes or no?'

She smiled at him, all her love in her eyes. 'I love you, Ransom Shaw, and, yes, I'll marry you as soon as you can arrange it. I have six years to make up for.'

That rakish smile tweaked at his lips as he swept her up ointo his arms. 'Since we're talking about making up time, let's go to bed,' he suggested huskily.

'Mmm,' Sam sighed, slipping her arms around his neck and holding on. 'I like the sound of that.'

HARLEQUIN®
Presents

The world's bestselling romance series...
The series that brings you your favorite authors,
month after month:

Helen Bianchin...Emma Darcy
Lynne Graham...Penny Jordan
Miranda Lee...Sandra Marton
Anne Mather...Carole Mortimer
Susan Napier...Michelle Reid

and many more uniquely talented authors!

Wealthy, powerful, gorgeous men...
Women who have feelings just like your own...
The stories you love, set in exotic, glamorous locations...

HARLEQUIN®
Presents

Seduction and Passion Guaranteed!

Harlequin Historicals®
Historical Romantic Adventure!

From rugged lawmen and valiant knights to defiant heiresses and spirited frontierswomen, Harlequin Historicals will capture your imagination with their dramatic scope, passion and adventure.

Harlequin Historicals . . . they're too good to miss!

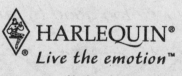

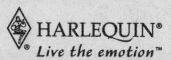

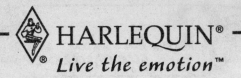